THE RULES THEY WROTE

Olivia Claire Dawson
@Copyrighted Material 2025

Dear Reader,

Before you begin, let's be clear. This book is not here to comfort you. It was born from years of therapy, years of peeling back the darker corners of my own soul, and from watching how hunger for power to lead, to submit, to control, quietly shapes every part of life: at work, at home, in love.

Don't mistake this for a book about sex. Yes, there's sex here. But the real story is what lies beneath: the machinery of dominance and surrender, of people who give, who take, and who pretend they're balanced when they're not.

Some of you will hate this book. You'll slam it shut, curse my characters, maybe even leave a one-star review to wash your hands of them. That's fine. This was never meant to please everyone. It's raw. It's unfiltered. It refuses to paint over the things most people would rather not see. Think of it this way: Fifty Shades cracked the door. This book rips the wallpaper off the walls inside that room. No whips, no chains, no leather clichés. What you'll find here cuts far deeper: psychological games, shame and control, choices that wound in ways no bruise ever could.

At its core is one woman, forced to ask the questions most of us spend a lifetime avoiding: Who am I? What do I want? This is not romance wrapped in roses. This is love as it really is: messy, strange, cruel, breathtaking. Some of you will devour it. Some of you will throw it across the room. Some of you will leave and then come back, restless.

Richard Pollak sat at its peak. Julian's hands trembled slightly as he stepped out of the car. She gave him her look—that look—sharp, silencing, commanding, and they walked to the door. In the grand foyer, they were greeted by Richard himself and a life-size portrait of Angela, Richard's wife—a striking, almost regal image that commanded the space. Julian knew it very well because he'd taken it himself a few weeks earlier, after Claire had mentioned to Richard that her husband was a professional photographer. Richard, looking for the perfect birthday gift, had seized on the idea. Now the piece hung here, framed like a shrine, as if to proclaim what Angela meant to him or perhaps to mask what she didn't. Julian's throat tightened as he took it in. That shot had been one of the hardest of his career. Even now, he could still remember the faint scent of her skin, the heat of the lights, and Richard's quiet breathing right behind him.

The evening, outwardly, was a success. Claire drank more than she intended, though no one could tell. She was skilled at that. She could preserve poise under the influence. Julian, by contrast, drank little. She knew why. Alcohol blurred him, made his speech fray at the edges. He needed all his faculties tonight.

PROLOGUE

Six Months Earlier

The dinner was extravagant. Claire felt something inside her flatten when Richard Pollak, the President of the bank where she worked, offered her the promotion to Vice President of Operations and then, in that smooth, calculated way of his, invited her to dine at his home. His wife would be there. So would Claire's husband, Julian.

It was unheard of. Richard never invited subordinates into his house. Claire was likely the first. She remembered the moment they turned into the long, pine-flanked driveway of his estate. The air smelled of money and groomed power. She turned to Julian.

"Be very nice. Make a good impression. Behave."

Julian tensed. "When don't I?" She caught something in his eyes. Hesitation, maybe even fear.

Julian was a photographer. Talented, understated. He barely made one-tenth of what she did and lacked the armor she had been forced to grow. Claire was now part of the bank's upper crust.

For myself. For finding the courage to be honest.

If you're not ready, close the book. But if you are, step inside. Welcome to these pages where masks crack, power shifts, and love bares its teeth.

Consider yourself warned.

Olivia Claire

Richard and Angela never cared and drank with abandon. Wine flowed as though extinction were imminent. Richard's jokes were easy, charming, but never careless. He remained the dominant presence in the room, not letting the mood slip out of his grip. Claire admired him for it. That kind of weight in a man that she was drawn to. Not the physical weight alone, though Richard was a large man, almost formidable, not overweight, just solid and fit. His body carried consequence. He looked like a retired linebacker with a PhD.

Julian was his opposite. He was slightly under six feet, wiry, quiet. He moved like a runner, light on his feet, muscles lean and long. He had the body of someone who fled, not fought.

Angela, the real one, was striking, tall, with sunlit hair and the frame of an ex-volleyball player whose body still remembered every drill. She was built to be looked at, exactly as the photograph promised.

Claire was forty-eight at the time. Julian, a year younger. Richard, just above fifty. Angela's age was hard to place. Probably younger than Claire, though she looked ageless in that calculated, expensive way. Stunning, of course.

Three adults. Polished and successful. Plus Julian. The dinner was a glossy portrait of high-functioning adulthood, except for one thing. Claire noticed something. Not about Richard or Angela. They were predictable. But about her own husband. It came in pieces, subtle and precise. Her glass kept filling. Her mind kept loosening just enough to notice what she had missed for years. Julian wasn't posturing. He wasn't trying too hard. But he was kind of reacting, and reacting to Richard. It happened when Richard stood behind the counter, slicing into a lavish cut of beef with a blade so sharp it whispered through the meat. A sleek, big, brutal Japanese knife. He looked over his shoulder.

"Grab that dish on the counter, will ya?"

The request was casual, almost offhand. Almost nothing deliberate about it. But Julian moved like a man under command. Too quick to stand, too eager in his stride, too pliant in the way he handed the dish over.

Claire blinked. Sipped her wine. Watched.

Julian was ready. The kind of readiness that betrays something deeper, something long-embedded, instinctive. Her gaze sharpened. Then Richard clapped Julian on the shoulder. "That's my boy." Angela giggled quickly, almost salaciously, and Julian smiled softly, sheepishly. There was something in his eyes, a faint glint of a shared memory that Claire didn't recognize. She stopped breathing for a second. A strange image entered her mind, unannounced, transparent as glass. Julian, on his knees before Richard. Hands shaking, working the zipper on the man's trousers. She didn't look away. The wine hummed in her blood, and for a moment, reality blurred with a darker kind of clarity. One that didn't need proof. Only recognition.

In that quiet instant, Claire understood why her marriage had never worked. She saw how Julian froze for a moment when tapped on the shoulder. Silent, waiting for punishment or praise, like a lab, tail twitching, primed before its master.

Or maybe it was the wine. Of course, no one knelt. In reality, Julian smiled his polite smile and simply moved on, happy to assist the host with the meal. A normal gesture. Human. Reasonable. Polite.

Maybe it was Claire's sick imagination. Or her perception of Julian. Or something older, darker, less nameable. She couldn't say. The images came anyway, unbidden, insistent. Then the guilt arrived, sudden and physical. Tiny beads of sweat formed at the base of her neck and slid down her spine. How could she think that about her own husband? What was she seeing? How could she picture him doing what had just played out in her sick mind? And worse—had she wanted him to? Had it excited her?

The fog in her head pressed inward. Questions rose, circled, collapsed into silence. Her thoughts felt trapped, as if trying to scratch their way out. Still, somewhere inside, clarity pulsed. She had seen something. And it mattered. Julian was a good man. She did not doubt that. But not the right one. Not for her, because goodness without resistance felt strangely hollow.

Chapter 1

Julian would've hated this place. Claire sat in the bar. Clean, easy jazz poured from the speakers — old melodies, almost forgotten. It was a hotel lounge in Jamaica, and she was alone. For the first time in her life. No Julian. No Chloe.

Chloe was in her third year at university in Boston and showed no signs of returning home. She hadn't taken the separation hard. Most of her friends had parents who'd drifted apart when the kids left for school. Chloe understood that. And there was no talk of divorce, no paperwork, no lawyers. Just a clean split. Claire had moved into a newly rented, flashy condo. Julian stayed in the house.

She took a sip of straight rum. Dark, unfiltered. It tasted fantastic. She preferred it neat, no ice, no distractions. Like now. Nothing softened. Her thoughts drifted, uninvited, back to the separation. It had happened about a month after that dinner with Richard and Angela. Julian hadn't understood. She'd failed to explain.

They had waved goodbye to their hosts, thanked them for the third or fourth time, and got into the car. Julian, suddenly relaxed and eager to please, had looked at her. "So, how did it go?" he asked.

She hesitated. Thought about answering. Then didn't. He glanced at her a few more times, waiting. But when no answer came, he let it go. He didn't press. He never did. Just drove. Claire watched the night traffic through the window, biting her lip, still feeling the wine in her bloodstream. The dinner clung to her skin. It wasn't the food or the wine or the way Angela had laughed with her whole throat, no, it was what she saw. Julian.

He had smiled too easily. Agreed too quickly. Jumped to help when Richard asked, like a junior employee scrambling to impress the CEO. It hadn't been dramatic. But it had been clear. Claire had seen it in his body language, his tone, the way he nodded, not to connect, but to obey. And it wasn't new. That was what hit hardest. It had always been there. Julian had always deferred to her, to others, to life. The marriage had functioned because Claire had done the steering, and Julian never questioned the map.

She had spent years wondering what wasn't working, why sex with him felt... performative. When she craved tension only to find servicing. Over the years of their marriage, sex had devolved from Julian's forgettable performances into something mechanical—him working dutifully between her legs. She had neither the strength nor the will to fix it. Maybe she didn't want to. Maybe, deep down, she knew it couldn't be fixed. She had blamed herself. Her stress, her control. But now, in the residue of beef, red wine, and Angela's immaculate lipstick, something inside her clicked. Julian wasn't the wrong partner by accident. He was the wrong man by design. She watched the headlights smear across the windshield, her lip caught between her teeth. And then, when they pulled into the driveway, the engine humming down, she turned to him, voice steady, no longer forcing the question back.

"Would you have given Richard a blowjob if I had asked you to?" she asked calmly, watching his face. It took him a full second, maybe two, to register the question. "What?" he said.

"You heard me," she replied, sliding her hand between his legs. She felt the response instantly. And in that moment, she knew her marriage was over. He tried, later. Raised his voice. Called her crazy. Told her she was imagining things. But she wasn't.

Now, sitting alone with her rum and the calming jazz, she could see things clearly— the dull edge in their sex life, the constant sense of being off, almost good, but not quite. Always circling the spark, never finding it. Their intimacy was like a luxury car, polished and intact, but with no fuel. Serviced regularly, but never driven. She hadn't ended the marriage with that question. She had only revealed it was already over. Julian never pushed, never demanded, but somehow she'd ended up exactly in the life that suited him best, with her out front, and him always in the shadows. All her life, she'd sensed Julian's quiet yielding, but standing so close to Richard, she finally saw it for what it was — the missing force she had always wanted in a man. Even then, after that question, he didn't erupt. He retreated. Left her alone in the echo of her own words. That was Julian's way in everything, not to fight, but to make her feel the full consequence of what she'd done.

***

The rum worked slowly, like a hand gliding down her spine, soft at first, then certain. Claire watched the flow of bodies in the bar, the easy vacation flirtations, the lazy smiles. She wasn't looking for a hookup. Not really. And she definitely wasn't looking for a relationship. She wanted something rarer. Discovery. Of herself. Of men.

Claire had only ever been with one man. Julian. A few brief university romances hardly counted as real experience. It wasn't that she hadn't fantasized about other men. Of course, she had. Passing glances, dirty thoughts, late-night cravings built around strangers in suits or jeans or nothing at all. Richard, too... her boss. Big. Serious. Commanding. The kind of man who'd wandered into her fantasies more than once, uninvited and entirely welcome. But she'd stayed faithful. Until the end. Until there was no more "them" left to be faithful to.

It took her a month to move out, and another five to learn how to live alone. She concentrated on her work, convincing herself, over and over again, that she'd made the right choice. Nearly six months passed without so much as a touch, without sex of any kind. Then one day, she decided that enough was enough. She needed a serious distraction. And she needed orgasms. So she took two weeks off. Left the bank, the cold late winter condo, the polite, probing messages from Julian, and flew to Jamaica. She'd had three dates in seven days. Disasters, all of them.

The first was Jack, a guy from Texas, in line at the beach bar. He offered to buy her a mojito. She accepted. He had decent shoulders, an attractive smile, and the kind of tan that said he was chasing something. Maybe youth. Maybe validation.

Dinner followed. That was her mistake. Jack talked endlessly. About cigars. About Cuban trade. About the differences between single malt and blended scotch. About a senator he once met. Claire timed it: forty-five minutes in, and he had yet to ask her a single question. He didn't talk to her. He performed near her. His tone was gentle but rehearsed, the way men sound when they think they're being charming. The eyes gave it away — glassy, self-absorbed, scanning her face not to read it, but to wait for his next cue. They were the eyes of a man who'd memorized three Wikipedia articles and thought that counted as depth.

She barely made it to dessert. Somewhere between his explanation of economic sanctions and the cigar lounge he wanted to open "once things chilled out politically," she excused herself to the washroom.

In the mirror, she saw it: the face she used to wear at board meetings when someone repeated her point in a deeper voice and got praised for it. When she returned to the table, she clutched her stomach.

"Something I ate," she said. "I should probably lie down."

Jack looked stunned. He hadn't even tried to flirt. He thought his voice was enough. She forgot about him before the elevator reached her floor.

The second date wasn't even a date. It was just a bar encounter right here, in fact, at the same table Claire was now occupying solo with her rum. Liam had looked at her the way men do when they're sure you've already said yes in your head and then asked if he could join her. She decoded the message in milliseconds, smiled, and said yes. He was tall, tan, and striking. The kind of handsome that made women look twice, and then regret it. His shirt was unbuttoned to the navel, as if his chest hair held the answers to life. It didn't.

The first thing he shared, certainly without any prompting, was his recent divorce. The second was that his ex-wife hadn't appreciated his charisma. The tone made it clear she was to blame for everything. Claire took her side instantly.

Next came a humblebrag about how successful his dating life had been post-divorce, though the word "successful" sounded suspiciously like "shallow and desperate." Only after that did he ask if she wanted another drink. She made another mistake: she said yes again. By the second sip, Claire had him classified. Emotionally exhausting. A high-end narcissist, expertly disguised as a confident man. Liam was deeply invested in himself, his tan, his smile, his imagined magnetism. She could feel him watching her for confirmation, convinced she was mentally undressing him, convinced she was already picturing the wild, meaningless sex he assumed he was best at. But Claire wasn't. Liam, she realized, was like a wine barrel after bottling, rich on the outside, empty inside. When she said she should be going, he took his drink, gave her a tight, confident smile, and said, "Well... let's finish these upstairs."

Claire pushed her glass away gently. "Some drinks," she said, "are better left unfinished." He blinked. Twice. She left. When she saw him at breakfast the next morning, he didn't manage so much as a hello.

And then there was Jason. Claire had been up early, craving strong coffee and a lazy walk along the beach before the heat settled in. She spotted him in the empty coffee shop alone, staring out the window like someone waiting for a message from the universe. There was a certain poetry to his posture, the kind women are trained to interpret as depth. She couldn't help herself.

"You don't look like someone enjoying the hotel... or the vacation," she said lightly.

He turned and gave her a perfectly rehearsed sad smile, the kind with enough world-weary charm to suggest a devastating backstory.

"You're very observant," he said. "Yeah, I'm in the middle of a crisis."

There it was. The crisis line. Claire had heard it before from men who always seemed to be in the middle of something: a breakup, an existential spiral, a complicated period of self-reflection. It was never resolved. That was the story. That was why he had that haunted look, like a man who'd lost something important and now expected every woman he met to help him find it.

They walked the beach together. He told her about his girlfriend. The heartbreak. How he'd "turned the page," but the pain still lingered. How hard it was to be open again. It was all so heavy, so beautifully constructed to draw empathy. Claire listened. She didn't interrupt. She was curious how far he'd take it. By the time they reached the rocks, she understood. Jason was the kind of man who wouldn't make a move, not directly. He always banked on the hope you'd lean in out of sympathy. She knew the type. A man who needed women to carry the emotional load, who asked for connection but offered only grief in return. He wasn't loud. He didn't perform like the others. The kind of man who seemed deep, but what he really wanted was a soft place to drop his sorrow, like a stone into someone else's well. Claire wasn't that well. She told him he seemed kind, that she hoped he'd find peace. She used the words that end things gently. And then she left him to suffer in someone else's arms. Someone who might mistake that kind of burden for intimacy. She wouldn't.

***

A voice behind her broke the spiral of Claire's thoughts. "Forgive me, but... the look on your face... It's either heartbreak or the start of something braver." Claire looked up. The woman standing there was breathtaking, though a strand of hair clung stubbornly to her lip, which she brushed away with the smallest, almost nervous flick of her fingers. Graceful, but not immaculate.

"I didn't mean to intrude... unless you'd let me?"

Claire smiled, intrigued. "Sure. I'd love company."

The woman slid into the seat across from her, drink in hand. It looked like a pale rosé. Delicate and untouched in the glass. "Amanda," she said with an invisible shadow of sadness in her eyes.

"Claire."

Amanda studied her with a gentle, almost reverent focus. Her body was not quite relaxed, her gaze was soft and slightly averted, with the stillness of someone waiting to be allowed in. "You looked... far away," she said softly. "I was worried you might vanish before I had the courage to say hello."

Claire let out a quiet laugh. "I'm actually glad you did. I just..." She paused, shaking her head, "...finished dissecting my recent dates."

Amanda tilted her head. "Anything left of them?"

"Spectacular failures," Claire said, smiling into her glass. Amanda chuckled, her eyes a sliver from direct eye contact. "Thank you for being that honest. It's... grounding." She hesitated, just enough to signal thoughtfulness. "May I ask, are you here alone?"

"I am." Claire nodded. "Took some time off. Separated for half a year now." Amanda's expression didn't shift, but her eyes reacted with sincere attentiveness. "I hope that wasn't too forward of me?"

Claire gave a slow shrug. "Not really." She paused. "I am just... discovering the world. Starting with the disappointing parts."

Amanda nodded, her voice almost hopeful. "Would it please you if I bought you a drink?"

Claire's smile curled, slow and knowing. "Do I have to sleep with you then?" Amanda laughed, warm, authentic, a hint of invitation beneath it. "Only if that's what you decide."

"Rum. Straight," Claire said with more statement than request, the words slipping out with effortless and surprising finality. Amanda rose without hesitation. Claire watched her walk to the bar, composed, fluid, as if responding to something deeper than words. For a second, barely more than a blink, Claire's eyes followed the movement. Controlled. Elegant. It really was something to look at. And in that same instant, discomfort, shame, and a flicker of fear swept through her, sharp with the sting of being caught wanting what she had never dared allow herself to want.

Amanda returned with the rum, placing it in front of Claire with almost ceremonial care. "I chose the best they had," she said. Claire's smile was almost indulgent. "Of course you did. Thank you." For reasons she couldn't yet name, Claire felt a ping of satisfaction like a service had just been rendered exactly as it should be.

She noticed Amanda hadn't touched her own glass of rosé. Claire lifted hers slightly.

"To you," she said.

Their glasses clinked with the faintest chime. Claire took a sip with no rush. "Beautiful," she murmured, then glanced across the table. "Are you here alone, too?"

Amanda nodded. "Yes. I work for a marketing agency. We had a corporate event here last week. Everyone else has already gone back, but I stayed a couple of extra days. To unwind. Going back early tomorrow."

Claire nodded, but her gaze lingered. Something about the woman intrigued her. Amanda looked a few years younger, early forties, maybe. Ridiculously beautiful. The kind of woman men twisted themselves into knots for. And yet... she didn't carry that like a weapon. No vanity, no performance. Claire couldn't place her. Her beauty felt almost incidental, like she didn't rely on it.

Where are you from?" Claire asked.

"Portland, Oregon."

"Beautiful place." Claire let the compliment drift, then asked, without ceremony, "Are you married?"

The question came too fast, but Claire didn't feel the need to apologize. Something about Amanda invited that kind of gentle claim.

Amanda's fingers tightened on the stem of her glass, a faint tremor betraying her before her voice steadied. "No," she said softly. "I... was with someone. For a few years. But he moved on." Her pause felt loaded, heavy with a sad story behind it. She reached for her glass, rolling the stem between her fingers as if weighing her next words. When they finally came, they detonated in Claire's mind. "...To his next sub."

Claire blinked. "Excuse me?"

Amanda lowered her gaze. There was no shame, only a kind of trained composure. "I served," she said, almost in a whisper. "Special relationships. Like in Fifty Shades... but... real."

"Oh," Claire said, slowly. Ah, that's what it is, she thought. That's the stillness, the receptive silence, the obedience. Amanda lifted her eyes, carefully searching Claire's face for judgment. There was none.

"That's interesting," Claire said. Her voice had changed slightly, become lower, more settled, like something had aligned. And then, without meaning to, her mind rushed backward. That listening posture, the careful tone, the waiting, the eyes searching for her word. She had seen it before, hadn't she? For many years. In Julian. Claire hadn't named it then. But now, seeing it in Amanda, so gently displayed, it all made sense. Then, surprising even herself, she asked:

"Tell me, how does it all work?"

Amanda smiled faintly, as though the question was inevitable, as though she had been waiting for it. "It's not about strict rules. It's more like... knowing where you belong. For some of us, it only happens when we're near someone who... has a kind of gravity. You feel it, and it steadies you. Like, okay, this is where I stop fighting."

Claire leaned back, her glass turning slowly in her hand. "So you're saying it's a need. Not a preference."

Amanda's eyes flickered up to meet hers, then down again. "A need. Yes. And a dangerous one, I suppose. It pulls you the way casinos pull people. The thrill, the risk, the surrender to chance. Except here... the stakes aren't money. They're much higher."

A few seconds of silence passed between them, charged but graceful. Then Claire's voice had gone quieter, almost confessional. "In my marriage, I was always the one who did the steering. I made the choices, I managed the details, even in bed.

He... simply followed. He never resisted, never claimed anything. At the time, I told myself it was a partnership. But looking back, I think it was something else."

Amanda tilted her head, listening. "So why did you end it?"

Claire let out a slow breath, heavy. "One night, we were at my boss's house for dinner. And I saw something in Julian that..." She trailed off, shaking her head as if to push the thought away.

Amanda leaned in slightly. "That what?"

Claire hesitated, biting her lip, fighting herself. Then, with a bitter laugh that wasn't really laughter at all, she said, "God, I can't believe I'm telling you this."

Amanda's eyes stayed soft. "You can."

Claire glanced down at her drink, swirling it once before speaking. She searched for words, biting her lip. "That night... I asked Julian something I never should've asked. Something ugly. "I asked him... the most arrogant, blunt question I've ever asked another human being. Whether he would give my boss a blowjob if I told him to."

Amanda didn't move, didn't even blink. She simply waited.

"And before he could answer," Claire whispered, "I already knew the truth." She looked up, her eyes wide, searching, doubtful. "Maybe I imagined it. Maybe I was drunk, or cruel, or seeing what I wanted to see. I'll never know. But in that instant, it felt true. I couldn't unsee it. And all I wanted was out."

Amanda nodded and fell silent. She chose not to comment or ask further questions; she felt like she had no right to. Then she said, "I saw you the night before. At this bar with a man."

Claire blinked. "You did?"

Amanda nodded. "You weren't trying. That's what struck me. You didn't try to be commanding or magnetic. You simply... were. Strong, focused, certain. You occupied the room. It was clear who set the terms of the exchange. That kind of presence doesn't hide, Claire. It radiates."

Claire felt heat creep under her skin, a mixture of pride and something else she refused to admit. "And you," she said slowly, "you seek that kind of presence, don't you?"

Amanda didn't answer at first. She let the question breathe, suspended, before replying with a candor that felt both intimate and dangerous. "Yes," she whispered. "I seek it. I crave it. Because when I find it… I can finally stop fighting myself. I can fall into that current and know exactly where I belong."

Claire breathed out, feeling her heart racing in her chest. Something stirred in her, unsettling and almost unbearable. Had she been this? A dominant? The word caught in her mind, too blunt, too foreign, but the question remained. She thought of Julian: the years of him cooking, cleaning, tending to Chloe, waiting for her to decide what was needed. She remembered how often he would look at her in restaurants, letting her choose the wine, the meal, and the pace of the evening. At the time, she had called it a partnership. Fairness. A balance. But was it? Was it leadership disguised as compromise? And what about in bed? His eagerness to please, to serve her… But then, when she saw that eagerness laid bare at Richard's, she recoiled from it. Or did she? Perhaps it wasn't disgust at all, but the sharper urge to press him down further, to claim him utterly, to make him hers in the most absolute way. She couldn't tell.

She had thought herself practical, organized, the one simply willing to carry the burden. But now, with Amanda sitting across from her, that neat story frayed. What if it hadn't been practicality at all? What if it had always been her hidden desire to direct, to be served, to receive without asking?

The thought made her swallow hard. She wasn't ready to claim it. Not yet. The word dominant felt alien, too sharp and final. But the hesitation itself, the fact that she was wavering, felt like its own confession. And that made the possibility all the more dangerous, because Claire wasn't ready to confront the darkest corners of her soul.

Chapter 2

Breakfast was crowded and loud, but Claire barely noticed. The clatter of plates, the hum of tourist chatter, blurred beneath the surface of her thoughts. In front of her sat a cup of coffee gone lukewarm and a perfect croissant she hadn't touched.

Last night was still in her body. They had talked until nearly 2 a.m., tucked in the corner of the hotel bar, warm light low, shadows stretching between their words. Amanda had told her everything. How she had discovered, years ago, her submissive nature not by accident, but as a kind of revelation. Her peace was in surrender, the joy was in obedience, and the pleasure was in knowing someone else was in control. And then came the man who understood her, guided her, and mastered her to perfection. For years, she had been happy until he released her. He let me go, she had said.

She had obeyed, of course. Submission meant listening, even to endings. Since then, she had been searching. Perhaps not even for love, but for a home. For direction. For a leash she could trust.

Claire's thoughts had kept drifting to Julian. Again. Now she knew better. He did not lack the ability to lead; he lacked the appetite. Listening to Amanda's story, Claire felt something awaken in her, dark, perilous, but sweet beyond reason.

As they left the bar, Claire noticed Amanda walking half a step behind. Silent, respectful, compliant, but so natural. Like a loyal dog at her heels. The elevator arrived, and they stepped in. Amanda's floor came first. As the doors slid open, she paused, turned, then slowly sank to one knee. Without words or performance, she took Claire's hand and pressed her lips to it, slow, reverent. Claire panicked, froze, breath locked in her chest. She had no idea what to do. Amanda rose slowly, gracefully, her eyes lowered, whispered a barely audible "Goodnight," and was gone.

The doors slid shut, sealing Claire in a narrow box of gold light. Her palm tingled, her body shivered with adrenaline. Oh, fuck! That wasn't a kiss. That was an offering. And the worst part was how much Claire liked it. Her throat tightened. This wasn't her. She didn't let people kneel for her. She didn't feel... this. But her body didn't care. Heat spread, quick and low. Her breath deepened. She pressed the hold-door button with one hand, as if keeping the world out, and with the other... moved lower, precise, desperate, aching for pleasure and the sharp, new truth rising inside her. She came in under a minute. Alone. Breathless. Eyes closed.

She didn't sleep for hours after that. The charge of it was electric, intoxicating, but shadowed by the hot, prickling shame of what it meant. The only comfort was knowing Amanda would be gone in the morning. Or so she told herself.

She looked down at her coffee now, deciding whether to finish it or ask for a fresh one. Her mind drifted to that dinner six months ago. Richard's gestures. Julian's reactions. And now… Now, Amanda's story. For the first time, she could answer the question that had haunted her marriage. She pushed the cup aside and stood, scanning the restaurant. Noise, color, silverware on porcelain. Steam from coffee machines. She needed something stronger. She turned toward the door. She needed a drink.

Chapter 3

Julian woke early, as he did every morning, and his eyes went straight to her side of the bed. Empty. It was always empty. No exceptions. As if, by some miracle, one morning, he might find her there again. The anger had faded somewhere between the silent repetitions of his days. The shock of her leaving had dulled. But the pain… that stayed. It sat heavily in his heart and followed him into every morning.

Julian walked barefoot to the kitchen. Pushed the button on the coffee machine. Let the hum and hiss fill the silence. The place was spotless, just as it always was now. Claire had been messy, not in a sloppy way, but in a fast, careless way. She almost never cooked, yet could create chaos in the kitchen within minutes, with clutter, spills, and a disorganized arrangement of half-finished things. He used to mutter about it under his breath, never aloud. Now he enjoyed the spotless.

He still tried to understand why she'd left. The question lived in him like a splinter. He kept circling back to that night. That dinner. The moment she'd asked him that question.

In the first weeks, he hated everything about it. He hated Richard, Angela, and Claire's new job. But slowly, he turned the lens on himself. Julian had grown up in a quiet, proper family. His mother, a high school teacher, was strict, structured, and demanding. His father, a music teacher at the local academy, was gentle, absent-minded, and more at home in a score than in a conversation. Julian had spent most of his time with his mother. She taught him how to clean, cook, keep order, and be responsible. From his father, he inherited the artistic streak. He discovered photography in his teens and stuck with it. Never a sporty kid, never a fighter, never one for conflict, he was the kind who kept the peace, who listened.

He met Claire at a photography event. She was striking, arresting in a way that felt almost architectural. She was so photogenic that it made him raise his camera without thinking. He took a few secret shots, then found the courage to approach her. To his surprise, she found him cute. And, somehow, she stayed. He kept her orbiting him in a subtle, almost invisible way, using photographs and art to set the rhythm, to tilt the axis, to bend her path toward his gravity. One day by the lake, with the wind catching her dress, he captured the sexiest shot he'd ever taken. When he showed her the image on the camera's screen, she said Wow. Then kissed him. That night was their first time together, and, for Julian, the first real sex of his life. As expected, she thought she commanded it. He knew better.

The coffee was ready. Julian took his cup and sat by the window. Mornings were quiet now. Pointless. He'd stopped making breakfast. That was for her, and she was gone. At first, he thought it had to be the sex. Claire was at that age when desire sharpened, when a woman hit her peak before the pause. And he knew he hadn't delivered. Why else would she ask that question? That horrible, terrifying question. And worse, why couldn't he have controlled himself from getting hard that very second? He hadn't even seen it coming. It just... happened. Her question, filthy, thought-out, had reached into something deep in him, something planted before. It once pushed him past a line. Showed him exactly who held the power. Placed him, without doubt, where he belonged. Or had she simply known something she shouldn't have? He couldn't tell.

He'd never wanted the grind, the late nights, the stress that chewed people up. Better to let Claire thrive out there while he kept the home the way he liked it. Everyone thought she was in charge.

Maybe that was the point. Maybe that had been the point all along.

Sometimes, out of nowhere, he'd think of Angela. The way she held still for him in the studio that day, her gaze steady, almost daring. He'd spent hours perfecting the shot, adjusting light until her skin looked like porcelain. Richard had stood behind him, close enough for Julian to feel his breath when he approved the final frame. Everyone thought it was just a portrait. Maybe it was.

The coffee cleared his head, the way it always did. Still, some mornings, certain memories made the taste turn metallic. He'd push them aside and focus on Claire. She had asked the question, touched him there, and then walked away. She must have thought him weak. A man who could swallow a question like that. Or worse... answer it.

Perhaps she'd needed someone brutal. Someone like Richard. Powerful. Solid. A man who could fill a room just by standing in it. Julian wasn't that man. He was the kind, regular, soft-spoken type. Devoted. But without fight, without that loud, unshakable power. And the tragedy of it was that he could never change himself into the man Claire wanted.

Julian dressed without shaving, started the car, and drove to his studio. If he didn't fill the day with work, Claire would fill it for him. She always had. Even now, without meaning to.

***

Claire was walking through the hotel lobby toward the elevators when she spotted Amanda at the reception desk. Fuck. Checking out, she thought. She hesitated. Her cheeks burned red. She was unsure whether to approach, to speak, or simply let the moment pass. But before she could slip out of view, Amanda turned just in time to catch her. And smiled. It was a small smile. But the body language behind it changed everything. Claire recognized the signal immediately. It was hard to miss. The same unspoken language she'd seen exchanged between Richard and Julian that night. A shift in presence. A silent offering. A mouldable will.

Claire stopped. She lifted her hand in a casual wave. Amanda began walking toward her. She moved with purpose, stopping just in front of Claire, eyes lowered in deference.

"My flight got cancelled. Rescheduled for tomorrow," she said softly. "I had to extend my stay another 24 hours."

"I see," Claire replied, her mind racing ahead, measuring, testing, weighing. She could simply smile, nod, and let Amanda pass. Pretend last night hadn't happened. That would be the safe thing, the rational thing, the right thing to do. The version of herself she had always been would have chosen that. But Amanda was still standing there. Waiting. Patient. Ready. And something in her stillness sparked an ache Claire couldn't define. Maybe it was attraction, maybe recognition. This woman wanted direction. Needed it. And Claire, against all reasons, wanted to give it. She swallowed, pulse thudding in her neck. When she finally spoke, the sound startled her, low, steady, purposeful, a voice she barely recognized as her own.

"I'm heading to the beach in fifteen minutes," she said. Each word landed with intent. "I expect towels and cocktails ready when I arrive. And fetch masks and tubes. We're going swimming." Claire wasn't sure why she said it. Maybe because the ocean made everything honest, and she was done staying dry.

Amanda's eyes lit up. "Yes, Ma'am," she answered, voice almost breathless. Her eyes never rose. Claire gave her a single nod, then turned without another word and stepped into the waiting elevator. She didn't look back. Amanda had her instructions. But when the elevator doors closed, Claire's body shook with a huge surge of adrenaline.

***

The towels were laid out. The cocktails were chilled. The beach gear was stacked neatly beside two loungers, well shaded from the Jamaican sun. Claire expected it all to be there. But she hadn't expected how it would feel to see it done. A strange, uncomfortable pressure settled in her chest. Pride? Excitement? No, probably guilt. How could she have done this? To Amanda? Treated her like… what? A servant? A slave? Claire couldn't believe she was doing it. Part of her wanted to turn around, to walk back to her room, curl up with a book, and pretend this entire thread of her life had never been pulled. Forget these games, these roles. But another part, the part that had been quiet for too long, longed to play. To push. To see. Before she could decide, Amanda stepped forward from beside the sunbeds, holding out one of the cocktails. Silent. Present. Waiting. Claire accepted it. Took a slow sip. The rum burned gently, familiar now. She sat on the edge of the lounger. Amanda lowered in the sand beside her, not quite seated, not quite kneeling. But low enough to defer without drama.

"If you don't mind, Ma'am," she said softly, "I'd love to rub in your sun cream." Claire didn't respond. She felt the words lodge somewhere between her spine and her breath. This wasn't who she was. She gave orders at work, yes, but not in bathing suits. Not to women kneeling in sand. Then, slowly, she nodded. And kept sipping. She needed more alcohol. Amanda didn't look up except once. A flicker, for a split second. And Claire wasn't sure what she saw. Devotion? Or desire?

Amanda began. Gently. Professionally. Her hands moved with ease over Claire's shoulders, along her neck, her back, her thighs. Claire looked around, unsure what reaction to expect from others. But no one cared. There were a few people scattered nearby. A gay couple. Vacationers. Everyone caught in their own orbit. No one was watching, no one reacting. And maybe that was what disturbed her most. No one saw anything strange in it. Claire had never thought of herself as gay. Still didn't. This…Whatever this was, it wasn't about sex. It was about power. About ownership and control. She felt it more clearly now, not in her body, but in the way Amanda moved around her. Offered, anticipated, served. Claire's thoughts spiraled. Then dissolved in the heat and the liquor. She lifted her glass. "Another cocktail, please."

Amanda didn't hesitate. She simply handed Claire hers. Untouched. Waiting. Claire took it, drank. Her muscles softened. Her mind followed. Amanda finished rubbing in the last streak of lotion and paused. "May I go fetch more drinks, Ma'am?" she asked quietly. Claire nodded. Amanda rose and disappeared toward the bar. Claire leaned back into the lounger, glass in hand, pulse peaking. This wasn't a game anymore. And she wasn't sure she wanted it to be.

The day passed like a dream, unhurried, indulgent, and slightly unreal. They snorkeled in warm, crystalline waters, wandered barefoot along the shoreline, laughed at nothing, and sipped cocktails that tasted like heat and freedom. When Claire grew tired, Amanda massaged her feet with devotion, and Claire drifted into a half-hour nap, suspended between touch and sunlight.

At lunch, seated at a shaded corner table, Amanda never opened her menu. She waited, silent and expectant. Claire didn't ask; she simply ordered for both of them. Wine flowed. Conversation came in soft waves. Claire felt herself loosening more and more with every glass. That afternoon, they retreated to a cabana. Amanda gave Claire a full-body massage, long, methodical, and wordless. Claire slept through half of it. At no point did

Amanda cross a line. Her hands never drifted anywhere they shouldn't. There were no testing touches, no invitations. Only pure service. Controlled and masterful. She knew her place. She knew how to serve.

By the time the sun began to drop behind the horizon, Claire understood this had been one of the best days of her life. Later, in her suite, as she prepared for dinner, she summoned Amanda and simply gestured to the chair by the vanity. Amanda did her makeup and hair with such effortless skill that it startled Claire. She was stunning. More than that, she was transformed.

For dinner, Claire chose the Italian restaurant at the hotel. She didn't want to leave the property, didn't want to waste any time. Amanda would be gone by morning. They entered the restaurant together, dressed to destroy. Heads turned. Claire barely noticed. Her attention was locked on Amanda.

The dinner was spectacular. At one point, Amanda leaned in. "May I leave you for a few minutes?" Claire nodded, casual but firm. "Be quick. We're going for a walk."

While sipping her espresso after the meal, Claire noticed him. Dark-haired. Tall. Handsome in the effortless, dangerous way Italian men often were.

Confident, intense, dark eyes. White shirt, open collar. Sexy smile. He was seated with a woman, beautiful, sharp-featured, but his attention kept drifting to Claire. He watched her. Not constantly, but long enough. Curious, maybe intrigued. Maybe something more. Claire returned a few glances. She saw his smile widen. He'd seen something in her, perhaps something about the two of them. Amanda and Claire. The dynamic. The charge.

Then Amanda returned. They finished their coffees, stood, and left. Outside, the night wrapped around them like silk, thick, warm, but softer than the sunlit hours. The stars were scattered across the sky. Herbs from nearby bushes released their scent into the air. Wine lingered in Claire's blood. The beach was deserted. They reached a bench under a tree, half-hidden, half-lit by moonlight. The waves whispered to the sand. A breeze moved through their hair. Claire sat. Amanda remained standing. Waiting. Always waiting. Claire didn't speak. She lifted the hem of her dress, slowly, revealing bare skin beneath. No underwear. She looked at Amanda, eyes dark, voice breaking with desire. She hadn't come here for this. Hadn't come for anyone. But somehow, everything led to this moment. This silence. This offering. "You know what to do," Claire said. Then she closed her eyes and let herself fall.

Chapter 4

She didn't see Amanda the next morning. Instead, when she woke, a bouquet of flowers waited on the table beside a business card and an impossibly delicate gold-covered chain, five feet long, coiled like a piece of art. The card read, in precise, elegant handwriting: "Always at your feet. A." Claire stared at it. The whole thing felt surreal.

She'd been drunk last night, drunk on wine and on the afterglow of a day she had enjoyed far more than she could have imagined. She remembered opening her eyes and seeing Amanda's dark, perfect hair between her thighs. She remembered the smile spreading across her face, that sudden rush, electric and absolute, of making another woman serve her. She remembered how her hand had moved on its own, gripping Amanda's hair as she reached the edge, guiding her, controlling her, owning the final explosive moment. That... had been absolutely seismic.

She could still feel a trace of sweetness between her legs. But mornings are mornings. And in the morning, there is clarity. And shame. She had never expected to fall this low, never imagined herself exercising power in that way, using someone, apart from Julian, for her own pleasure.

And yet, she knew she never would have felt it at all if not for Amanda. Amanda had been the one to guide her into it, to show her how intoxicating power could be. To lift her and worship her.

Still, the shame burned. Claire was glad Amanda had gone, though she knew instantly she would miss her. She got out of bed, picked up the chain, and examined it. The meaning was unmistakable. If there were ever a next time, and there probably wouldn't be, this chain would have only one place to attach. A collar. Claire slipped the chain and the card into her bag, bent to smell the flowers, and headed to the shower.

***

The day dissolved into fragments, memories, stray reflections, sudden bursts of insight. Claire's mind craved clarity, and sometimes, in brief, sharp episodes, it came. There was no denying it. She had enjoyed her newfound role as someone who could exercise power. The realization both thrilled and worried her.

Regret seeped in, curling around her thoughts. Should she have been doing this with Julian all along? Making him serve her? But then, hadn't he already been serving her? She had just never called it that. He cooked. He cleaned. He took care of

Chloe all those years, freeing her to work late, to travel, to climb the bank's ladder until she was almost at the top. He never argued. Never resisted. Always did what she asked, without question. In bed, he was obedient, eager to please. He went down on her every time without needing to be told. It was as though he felt the need, almost an obligation. So why did it feel different with Julian, more unwelcome than desired?

Her memory jolted to a moment years earlier. His birthday. He had been careless with the champagne and got tipsy, loose, almost giddy. She was in the bathroom, removing her makeup, when he appeared in the doorway. Without a word, he knelt behind her, slid her underwear down in slow motion… and then… God, Claire still felt it, the shock of his tongue sliding into a place he had never touched before, a place she had never imagined he would go. Shame had flared hot and immediate. But she hadn't turned. Hadn't stopped him. They never spoke of it, and he never tried it again. Good, because the worst part was that she never wanted him to.

The next morning, her thoughts had settled. Slowly, the day with Amanda, the strange but sweet new role, the orgasm began to fade. Perhaps it was her usual guilt and shame, edging in and burning at the back of her mind, that pushed it away. She told herself it had been a life experience, a quest, a search for something new. Many people did it, she reasoned, trying to find their true selves. So had she. Did she like it? Yes. A lot. But it was over now. Time to move on. And yet, her mind kept circling back to the same questions: Who was she? What did she want from her life? Was she meant to give… or to receive?

The day flew by, and the night fell, but the air stayed heavy and unmoving, a humid blanket that clung to the skin. Claire wandered the hotel grounds, walking without purpose, thinking without resolution. Dinner had been skipped again; she'd had no appetite. Cocktails forgotten, too. Only a bottle of water in her hand, sipped slowly as she moved.

Ahead, the tennis courts blazed under floodlights, the steady thwack of rackets against balls echoing into the night. How can they play in this heat?, she thought as she drew closer. The gate swung open, and he stepped out. The man from the restaurant. But tonight there was no suit, almost nothing at all. Only tennis shorts, a T-shirt in one hand, a racket in the other. Sweat slicked his chest, muscles carved and tight. His breathing was rough, but his smile was unchanged. He recognized her instantly. "Hey," he said. "Spying on me?"

"Never crossed my mind," she replied. He laughed.

"You won't want to shake my hand. It's too sweaty. I'm Antonio."

"Claire." She said it simply, but her eyes had already gone to his chest. Solid. Sculpted. He noticed. "I knew you were Italian, " she said. He grinned.

"Where's your girlfriend?" he asked.

"She's gone. Early flight."

"Oh," he said, "so you're alone?" He asked, eyes intent. Claire met his gaze with the kind of challenge only a woman can give when she's daring a man to act. "But you're not." He shook his head, smiling. "That was my younger sister that night at the restaurant. She's getting married here in three months and wanted me to come with her to check the hotel out and make sure everything works. You know… second opinion."

"I see."

Something old moved in her heart—the fantasy man. The one who didn't ask. The one who took. The one she used to imagine finding her in some dark corner and making her his, without hesitation. Her pulse quickened. He stepped a little closer. Close enough for her to catch the clean bite of sweat on his skin, the faint musk of exertion. He was taller than she'd thought. The air between them seemed to shrink. She held his gaze a second too long.

"You look like you've been looking for trouble," he murmured.

"Maybe, I have," she said, clearly challenging him.

The corner of his mouth lifted. "Then you've found it."

Her body reacted before her mind did with the low thrum in her stomach, the catch in her breath. This was what she had imagined on lonely nights. Those rough hands. Claire's pulse quickened. She knew exactly what she was doing, and she wanted it. She wanted the danger, the rawness, the sharp taste of crossing a line. At least, she thought she did. When he caught her wrist and drew her off the path, she didn't resist. She didn't want to. The thrill was already humming. She let herself be pulled behind the line of bushes, out of the light, into shadow.

The push against the wall was hard, almost theatrical. She welcomed it at first, the pressure of his body pinning hers, the scrape of rough concrete on her palms. His mouth found her neck, hot and urgent. Her dress was yanked up, and her underwear was torn. Her mind whispered: Yes... this.

But then... The fantasy shifted. The smell of sweat turned sour. His breath was ragged but careless, impersonal, like he was somewhere else. His grip was holding her in place, restraining, not commanding. And somewhere between his breath and his body, the wanting drained away. Suddenly, she understood the difference. This wasn't power. This was force. He wasn't leading. He was simply taking what he wanted.

Amanda had made her choose to give. Julian had waited to be told. Both had understood, in their own ways, that the spark lived in the exchange of control, not its theft. Here, there was no exchange. No choice. The spark dropped out of her, fast as if a switch flipped. Heat gave way to cold. The wall behind her felt harder, the night air heavier. She kept her eyes closed, willing herself back into the fantasy, but it was already gone.

He pushed harder. She tensed. And then she did what women learn to do with perfect, practiced grace. She faked it. He believed it. Ten seconds later, it was over. She felt blood on her mouth. Must have busted her lip against the wall. He stepped back. She adjusted her dress, retrieved her bottle of water, and picked up her underwear, her legs unsteady. Blood stained her lip as she turned toward him.

His eyes widened. "Oh my God! Did I hurt you?" He reached for her face; she jerked away. "It's fine. Accident." She even managed a smile and added, "That was...umm... unexpected."

"Yeah," he said. "Can we—"

"I need to go," she cut him off. "Attend to my lip. Before it starts swelling."

"I'm so sorry."

Never mind." She waved him off and started walking. He caught up. "Breakfast tomorrow?" "Sure," she said simply, and stepped inside the building. Her voice had been calm, but her pulse still rattled in her ears. The air-conditioning hit her skin like ice, chasing away the last of his heat. She realized she wasn't trembling from what had happened. She was trembling from the clarity. She would never let anyone take her again.

Claire gripped the edge of the sink and stared at herself in the mirror. The bleeding had slowed, but her lip was swelling. Her face looked alien, hollow-eyed, as though something essential had been scraped out of her. Rage began to climb her spine, slow and hot. Her fingers curled into fists.

"What the fuck were you doing, Claire?" she asked the woman in the glass. "Hm? What the fuck were you thinking?" Her breath came in gusts, uneven, like wind rattling a window.

"You left Julian because he wasn't man enough. Because he didn't want you enough. And now what? You find out that being taken, wanted isn't for you either?" She leaned closer, her voice dropping to a whisper meant only for her reflection.

"Why did you have to humiliate Julian like that? That blowjob question... are you serious, Claire? The man did everything for you. For years. He raised your child. He's the father of your child, for fuck's sake. And look at you now—" Her voice cracked.
"Bossing another woman like a pet... then letting a stranger pin you to a wall."

The words burned her throat. "What is wrong with you?" Her voice rose to a shout before breaking entirely. Tears hit her cheeks fast, hot, unrelenting. She slid to the floor, knees giving way. Pain spread to every part of her body. Her life splintered, scattered right in front of her.

"What the fuck do you want, Claire?" she kept asking herself between sobs. But the answer never came.

Chapter 5

Her photograph covered the entire wall in his studio. The same photo he'd taken that day by the lake, the one that made her kiss him for the first time.

Julian sat at his desk. The day was slow, and the business was even slower. His schedule mocked him: one commercial shoot tomorrow, a high-profile wedding the day after, then nothing for nearly a week. It wasn't enough. Worse, Julian was terrified of the future and the looming reality of a legal divorce. What would he do without her? Without her income, her support? He knew he could never survive on photography alone. The years of pretending he was doing fine had crumbled. She'd never known the truth about his business, which in reality barely covered its costs. Soon, the studio would have to go because he wouldn't be able to sustain the rent. The thought made him physically sick.

He needed to do something if he ever wanted a chance of getting her back. But was that even possible? He'd thought about what she'd done to him thousands of times, maybe more. Turning it over like a stone in his hands, searching every side for a mark, a clue. He tried reading between the lines, but there was nothing there. Nothing bad had been brewing between them before that night. Before that question. He'd asked himself a thousand times whether she knew his secret. Some days, he was sure she did. Other days, clarity told him she didn't.

He'd searched the internet for articles, blogs, and forums. Anything that might explain her behavior. The closest he came was an essay on power games. Submission and dominance. Something in it clicked. Had she been steering him toward some darker form of dominance? Because the other kind, the unspoken kind, had been in place for years in their family. And it had been his choice, not hers, his perfect modus operandi.

He had always known his place with Claire. She was strong, resourceful, and blunt. A natural leader. She had climbed high in her career, earned more than he ever would. He accepted it, even admired it. Maybe he created it, too. To him, she had to be a dominant woman. He'd bent himself in ways she never saw. Done things, agreed to things, that kept her world spinning exactly the way he imagined she'd like. Some of those choices still lingered in him, part pride, part regret.

But then... she crossed a line. That was how he saw it—a line between love and something much colder. A line even someone willing to submit shouldn't be forced over. That question meant that she had wanted more. Something he wasn't willing to give for free.

The hope of getting her back burned in him day and night. He wasn't ready to move on, to close the chapter, to start a new one. He had always served without direct orders, without explicit words, still creating ways to make himself useful, to make himself hers. That was his investment in their marriage and his pursuit of a trouble-free life. Was it enough? Probably not.

If he had ever been like Richard, the marriage would have ended years earlier. Claire would never have tolerated a man stronger than her, certainly, not in the house, and never in bed. Julian had long since convinced himself of that. But was it true? He wasn't sure anymore.

The more Julian thought about it, the more a dangerous, almost shameful idea began to take shape. She had already asked for more once in that horrible, intentional question, and he had pulled back. But what if he didn't? What if there were no hesitation, no pride, no limits? He knew that feeling. He had stepped over that line before. What if he gave her the version of himself she might have been searching for all along: not only agreeable, accommodating, but entirely, consciously hers? His true version. The thought churned in him, part fear, part longing, part something darker. Would she come back if he gave her everything she asked for? Maybe she would. But Julian knew it wasn't that simple.

If he wanted her back, if he wanted his old life, his comfort, his lazy days and silence, the fortress of a house that shielded him from the world and her money, he would need to play a lot smarter than that. He needed to come up with something more than offering everything right away. More than surrender. More than acceptance. And Julian was no rookie at games like that.

He swallowed hard, trying to push it down, but it stayed lodged in his throat, stubborn and alive. His mind spun like an overworked engine. His fingers hovered over his phone. Then he began to type. *Hi. I'm sorry to bother you, but could I have a chance to speak with you in person?*

He paused, hesitated, then, finally, hit send. The status shifted from Sent to Delivered. Not read. Not yet. The message was crafted with care, worded to carry the shadow of his submissive side. Let her think he was ready to beg. The surprise would come later.

Reluctantly, Julian unlocked the storage. Dust, old photographs, discarded frames, boxes of bills, and bank statements cluttered the shelves. He dug through the mess until he found what he wanted: an old industrial landscape he'd shot years earlier for a client. Rough, soulless, impersonal. About the same size as Claire's portrait. He hauled it out and propped it against the wall. This would be the swap. The first domino that fell. The act she would notice. It took him nearly twenty minutes to hang it properly, his hands steady but his mind racing. She would eventually come to the studio, searching for him. She had the front door key. He knew that. And when she did, she'd see it.

Julian smiled to himself, caught up in the elegance of the move. The erasure. So caught up, in fact, that he forgot the simplest detail: relocking the storage. Or maybe he only thought he did. Stress had a way of blurring even the smallest things.

***

The following morning, Claire skipped breakfast. She checked out without lingering and headed straight for the airport. In the dark hours, when sleep refused to come, she'd changed her ticket online. She wanted out. Out of the games she had started playing, back to work, back to whatever her real self was.

But the last few days still haunted her. On the plane, Amanda's memory shoved aside Antonio's intrusion. It was Amanda who flooded her mind, Amanda who had given her the single happiest day of the trip. Every time Claire closed her eyes, she saw Amanda's dark head moving between her legs and felt the heat drying her lips. Amanda had somehow known exactly how she wanted it. Not perfect. More than perfect. Every movement of her tongue sent Claire higher, lifted her out of herself.

More than once, she took Amanda's business card from her bag, her thumb tracing the inked letters like a secret she wasn't ready to share. She almost sent her a text with a few words to keep the thread alive, to plant the seed of another meeting. Each time she slipped the card back into her bag, the ache sharpened instead of fading. The restraint was almost worse than the act would have been.

When she landed, a text message waited for her. From Julian. He wanted to talk in person. He'd have to wait, she decided. First, she needed to take care of herself. Give herself time. She had three more days off work. Outside the terminal, she slid into the backseat of a taxi and pulled out her phone. Scrolling through her contacts, she found the number. Dialed.

"Hi, Olivia. It's Claire. I have something urgent. Could you fit me in first thing tomorrow morning?" A pause, a voice in her ear. "Oh. I see. Fine. I can come now."

She gave the driver a new address, exhaled, and settled back against the seat. Now she was going in the right direction — to see her therapist.

***

Antonio sat in the armchair of his suite, elbows resting on his knees, head low, like a boxer after a fight he wasn't sure he'd won. The taste of her still lingered on his tongue, but so did something sharper. Unease.

Claire. When he'd first seen her across the restaurant, she'd been exactly the kind of woman who turned his head, not only beautiful, but composed in a way that made everything around her feel steady. She didn't fidget. She didn't try to be noticed. She simply sat there, but the room registered her anyway. She'd met his stares with that cool, almost amused glint in her eyes, and Antonio thought, there it is. The spark. That charge between two people who are about to step off the edge together.

So when he bumped into her at the courts and she came with him into the shadow of the wall, he'd read it as consent to the whole package, not only sex, but the kind of sex that came with an adrenaline rush. Not his everyday style, no. But it was a game he was willing to play when the partner wanted it. And she had wanted it, hadn't she?

Now, hours later, he wasn't so sure. Her busted lip... Jesus, that image wouldn't leave him. The look in her eyes afterward hadn't been fear, exactly, but it hadn't been joy either. He hated that. Hated the possibility that she thought he'd just taken what he wanted. That wasn't him.

He'd liked her. Not only her body, though that alone could have undone him, but her. The intelligence in her voice. The way she didn't flinch at his directness. He'd thought she was the kind of woman who wanted to taste danger, maybe live out a fantasy she'd never speak aloud. He'd thought he was giving her that. Now, he wondered if he'd ruined it.

He stood, restless, and paced the suite. Part of him wanted to go to the reception right now, find out her room number, knock, and explain himself. But the other part, his better judgment, knew how that could look. A man showing up at her door after the sex she might be regretting... No. He wouldn't risk making her feel cornered.

He'd wait until morning. He'd catch her at breakfast. Keep it light, even playful, to show her he liked her for more than the way she'd tasted, that he wasn't the asshole she might be replaying in her mind right now.

Morning came early for him. He dressed carefully, scanned the dining room from the entrance, and took a table with a view of the door. Every time it opened, he looked up. A family. Two men in golf shirts. A woman in a sundress. No Claire. He waited an hour, nursing a coffee that had long gone cold. Still nothing. Finally, he caved. At the reception, he leaned casually against the counter, giving the receptionist his best smile. "Hey, this might be an odd question," he began, "but I met someone here last night. A lovely American woman traveling alone. Early forties, long blond hair, green eyes. I wanted to leave her a note."

The receptionist thought for a moment, then said, "Oh. She checked out this morning. Took an early flight."

For a beat, Antonio didn't move. Then he nodded once, smiled like it was nothing, and thanked her. Out in the morning sun, he felt the dull pull settle in his heart. She was gone. And the worst part was not even that he wouldn't see her again. The worst part was knowing she might never understand that he hadn't meant it to be like that. Not with her.

***

The traffic crawled. Spring had only begun to breathe. Amanda had the window down, warm air drifting in as she drove home from work. Her first day back after Jamaica. And it had been a disaster. She had sat at her desk, staring at spreadsheets, but her mind had stayed under the Caribbean sun, right at the beautiful feet of Claire. She could still feel the faint press of Claire's toes curling against her thigh, the salt of her skin lingering at the back of her tongue. The woman she'd met. The woman she couldn't shake. A magnetic, irresistibly elegant force of dominance.

Amanda was confused. She had never imagined herself serving a woman. But maybe submission didn't have a gender, or at least that's what she told herself. Her past, traumatic as it had been, suddenly felt like preparation, training, an initiation into her own depths. All her life, she had ached to serve, in one form or another. When she discovered the world of dominance and submission, she dove in headfirst. But this was different. More dangerous. Sweet. Dark. And threaded with something she had never expected. Maybe love. What the fuck? Did I fall in love with a woman?

It felt strange. Unreal. Yet she couldn't deny the pull. She had no idea who Claire really was. She had no phone number, no email, no way to find her. Nothing but hope. That fragile, maddening thread she clung to in the dark. Amanda had left her business card and the gold leash, trusting that if Claire wanted her, she would summon her. That was the right thing to do for a good sub: wait. Be patient. But the waiting hurt. What if Claire never called?

She pulled into the lot of a small boutique market and went in, picking up a few delicacies and a bottle of wine. Tonight she would drink, watch a movie, and think of Claire. Her mind drifted back to her previous life, one that had belonged entirely to him. She had lived in cycles of waiting until the phone buzzed with orders to come serve. He lived alone, so she cooked, cleaned, and tended to him. Sometimes he took her right there in the hall, wordless, unapologetic. She always complied. She knew there were others. She had seen the evidence, expensive lingerie, ripped and discarded. Not hers. She never asked. Deep down, she wanted to be the only one, but fear kept her silent. Punishment had been regular. He called it training. And then, just like that, one day, as she knelt before him, he told her it was their last meeting. Tears had filled her eyes. That felt like another lifetime now. Today, she told herself, she was happier. If Claire called, she'd drop everything, job, friends, city, her old memories, and go crawling on her knees.

Chapter 6

Olivia Dayton crossed her legs, balancing the glass of water on the side table with an elegance that came from years of repetition. Those years had taught her to read between the lines, dissect pauses, inflections, and the subtle cracks that revealed where a truth was straining to surface. Claire had been her patient for nearly a decade. She had walked her through Chloe's adolescence, the politics at the bank, the steady climb to executive power. Never once had Claire suggested her marriage was anything but steady, if not exceptional. Until now.

This was different. This wasn't your everyday marital friction. This felt tectonic.

"Let me try to line things up," Olivia began, her voice calm and measured. "You've described a long marriage where your husband played a supportive, domestic, and willing role. You accepted it, maybe even relied on it, until that dinner. And at that dinner, something inside you broke loose. Instead of talking, you… tested him. In a way that shocked both of you."

Claire's shoulders tensed, as if bracing against a blow.

"Why that method?" Olivia asked gently.

Claire shrugged. "I was drunk."

"Yes," Olivia said, nodding slowly. "Alcohol blurs filters, but it doesn't invent motives. You reached for something very precise. Sexual. Humiliating. You didn't have to give him that test. But you did. Why?"

Claire's throat tightened. She stared at the rug, then muttered, "Because I already knew the answer."

"What answer?"

"That he'd... react. And he did." Her voice picked up speed, went on the defensive. "He got hard as soon as I asked him. You don't know Julian the way I do. I'd seen it for years, the way he deferred, the way he bent himself around me. That night just confirmed it."

Olivia's eyes softened, but her voice remained steady. "Claire... an erection isn't proof of identity. It's proof of arousal. Nothing more. If we accept your reading of the moment, then what you really did wasn't to confirm something about Julian. You confirmed something about yourself. About what you wanted to see."

Claire's lips parted, then closed again. Olivia let the silence hang, then said, "Let's put it this way: you didn't ask him about love, trust, or even marriage. You chose sex. Submission. That choice tells me this is not entirely about him alone. It's about the part of you that craved control but never spoke it aloud. Amanda only made you realize what you'd been circling all along."

Claire looked up at her sharply, but said nothing.

"And now," Olivia continued, "you say you left Julian because he never became the man you wanted. But listen to your own words, Claire. You had a man who cooked, cleaned, raised your daughter, and adored you. He never fought you for control. He bent willingly. You had, in effect, what Amanda gives you now. Only with him, you couldn't enjoy it. Why?"

The question landed hard. Claire's face flickered with something raw, a blend of recognition and refusal.

"I don't know," she whispered.

"Yes, you do," Olivia countered softly. "You wanted him to take you sometimes. To push back. To claim you. That's what you said. But when Amanda kneels, you don't call it a weakness. You call it power. You revel in it. So what's the difference?"

Claire swallowed, heat rising in her chest. Images of Amanda surged up uninvited, hair on her thighs, obedience given without a word, the delicious sense of authority that had thrilled and shamed her in equal measure. She couldn't name it yet, but something in her bones told her Amanda's kneeling was genuine, while Julian's eager submission had never been. Why, she couldn't explain.

Olivia watched the conflict move across Claire's face. Then, very carefully, she asked, "Tell me something, Claire. If Julian had agreed that night — if he'd said yes to your test, yes to everything — what would you have done with that answer?"

Claire froze. She had never thought that far. The room seemed to press in, smaller and tighter. "I... I don't know."

Olivia studied her for a long time. "You didn't expect him to agree," she said finally. "You weren't testing him. You were setting a trap you thought he could never walk into. That tells me you weren't only looking for the truth. You were looking for justification to leave."

Claire flinched, breath catching.

Olivia leaned back, her eyes steady. "One last thought. You tell me Julian was always yielding. But are you sure? Some people lead by retreating. By stepping aside. By letting you move exactly where they wanted you to go. If that's the case… perhaps you weren't the only one directing the marriage."

Claire blinked, throat dry. Her mind seized on the words, circling them like prey. She tried to answer, but only a hoarse whisper came out: "I've never thought about that."

***

The doorbell rang. Claire had just stepped out of the bathroom, hair wrapped in a towel, coffee in hand. She padded to the door, glanced through the peephole. Julian. Fuck. She'd forgotten to answer his text. She opened the door. He stood there, paler than she remembered, thinner, with the hollow look people get when something in them has been slowly eroding. Claire felt a strange jolt, regret, pity… or something else she couldn't find a word for, slip down her spine.

"Hi," he said.

"Hi. Sorry, I didn't answer your text. I've been busy…"

"That's okay," he murmured. "I won't take long."

She pulled the door wider. "Come in."

He shook his head. "No. I just wanted to…" He stopped, searching for words. "All these months, I've been thinking… about that. About what you asked me."

Claire tensed. She hadn't expected this. She didn't want to revisit that question.

"I've thought about it for a long, long time," he went on. "And… I love you, Claire. I always have. But… I would have never done it. Not for you. Not even if it cost me my marriage… which it did."

He lowered his gaze. "I just thought you should know. For closure. I've finally settled it in my head. I'm moving on. And… I wish you all the best."

He turned and walked down the stairs.

Claire stood motionless. Julian, her Julian, had just told her he wouldn't have done it, even for her. Wouldn't. She remembered the heat in him that night, the involuntary swell that had told an entirely different story. This was the man who used to move at her first word and sometimes at a glance. What changed? Another woman? Unlikely. Then why had it taken him six months to find his voice? And now, of all times, he was using it to... dismiss her? End things? Wish her all the best? She shut the door slowly, as if sealing something dangerous outside, and crossed to the chair. She needed to sit down, to steady herself. Her mind was a hive. She had never heard a "no" before. Now, with just a few well-placed words, he had stepped across a line, challenged her, and been brave enough to do it. For years, Claire had believed she was the one making decisions in the family. The separation — that was hers, wasn't it? The others, too. Or... were they? A troubling thought crept in: why did it feel like the separation was the only decision that had truly been hers?

***

Julian took the stairs two at a time, a current of almost giddy triumph surging through him. The performance had been near perfect. He'd seen it in her eyes—the flash of surprise, the way her composure faltered. He'd challenged her. He'd said 'No' for the first time in their shared history. More than that, he'd told her he was moving on.

Let her sit with that. Let it gnaw at her, settle deep in her heart where it would fester.

But the truth... The truth was deliciously different. Julian knew exactly what game he was playing, a slow-burn con meticulously thought through. God, yes, he would have given Richard a fucking blowjob if it meant saving his own world. But why show his hand when there was a better way to draw her back? No. Before he knelt down in front of anyone, he needed to rebel, to push back. Let her feel the ground shift beneath her feet, that illusion of control she'd held for years suddenly at risk. Let her believe she was losing him without ever seeing how skillfully she was being guided, how someone in the shadows had been shaping her life all along. Julian smiled to himself. The game was on, and he meant to win it. Moreover, he had tested something important, and now he knew she had no idea about his secret.

Chapter 7

The only sounds were the soft clink of cutlery and the low hum of the morning breeze. Breakfast was served on the veranda, sunlight spilling across white linen. Richard, working through a plate of Belgian waffles and sipping Prosecco, let his gaze linger on his wife. Angela was radiant, as always. Last night's performance still thrummed in his bones—mind-blowing sex. She was a fucking goddess. That was why she still sat across from him.

"You know, hon," he said between sips, "I've got a juicy bit of gossip for you."

Angela arched a brow, slowly licking a strawberry in a way that made him feel it low in his body. "Yeah?" she murmured, the invitation clear.

"Remember Claire and Julian?"

"The one who took that photo?" She smiled. "How could I forget?"

Richard's lips curved. "Exactly. How could you…" He let the pause hang. "I met with her yesterday about some bank business. She just got back from a two-week trip to Jamaica... Turns out she dumped him. Six months ago."

"Oh, did she?" Angela tilted her head. "That would be right after that dinner, wouldn't it?"

He nodded. "Yeah."

"Why'd she dump him?"

Richard shrugged. "Didn't say. Usual bullshit about 'growing apart.'"

"Oh, yeah, yeah. Everyone says that." She gave him a mischievous smile. He studied her face, catching the glint of devilish fire in her eyes. "What? Thinking about another photo shoot?" Angela's smile deepened as she plucked up another strawberry. Angela shook her head with playful dismissal. "How about her?"

Richard gave a low hum, feigning surprise. "If I make it happen, what's in it for me?" Her eyes narrowed, calculating, like a poker player weighing a call.

"I might change my mind... and let you have two pieces of the pie."

"Deal," he said, carving off another bite of waffle.

***

Claire sat forward in the chair, her body restless, shoulders tight, the coffee she'd carried in from the lobby already cooling on the side table. The sessions had become more than helpful. They were a necessity. Ten days had passed since Julian's visit, yet it still pressed on her like a boulder she couldn't shift. Thoughts of him, their life together, the choices she had made, unnerved her. She could no longer think straight on her own. Olivia noticed that. She let the silence breathe for a few moments before prompting gently, "Why don't you start where you left off last time?"

Claire exhaled sharply. "Julian. He came to my door. Said goodbye. Said he was moving on." She shook her head, quick and frustrated. "And now he's vanished. He's not answering his phone, not at home, not at the studio. I checked. He even took down my photograph. The one that hung there for almost twenty years. Replaced it with some… empty industrial scene. He's finished with me. That's his message."

Olivia let the words settle. "And what do you make of that?"

Claire's mouth tightened. "Maybe there's another woman. That would explain it." She hesitated. "But I can't picture him with anyone else."

Olivia leaned forward slightly. "Claire... you chose separation. You've pursued your own desires, your own experiments. Why would it surprise you that he might choose differently now?"

Claire opened her mouth, then closed it again. She stared at her hands. "In theory, yes. He has the right. But in practice—" Her voice caught. "In practice, I can't believe he slipped away this easily."

Olivia watched her. "So it isn't only about him being with someone else. It's about him existing outside of your reach. That's what feels intolerable."

The words hit harder than Claire expected. She blinked, slowly, before forcing a nod. "Probably. Yes. That's it... Maybe not. I am not sure."

Olivia gave a slight, measured pause. Then: "Still, his timing is unusual. To come after so long, deliver a speech about moving on, and disappear? It feels... exaggerated. Almost staged. What's your sense of that?"

Claire frowned. "Feels overdone, yes. Odd. Like he wanted me to believe something. But what? Look, he used to send me texts every single day after separation, he called, he asked how I was, he offered help with whatever..."

"That's the question," Olivia said softly. "Don't rush to an answer. Just notice that the gesture may not be as straightforward as it seemed."

Claire shifted, thinking. Olivia let her sit with it, then steered gently. "Now, you also mentioned Richard. Tell me why that meeting has stayed with you."

Claire hesitated. "It was strange. Richard never talks about personal lives, never. But a few days ago, after business, he asked me about Julian. About the separation. About Jamaica. He wanted details. Pressed, almost. And for him, that's… unusual."

"What did you tell him?"

"The usual story. Grew apart. Empty house after Chloe left. Nothing specific."

"And still you're bothered."

"Yes." Claire's voice sharpened. "Because it felt like more than curiosity. Like he wanted something from me. And when I think back... that dinner comes up again. He was too assured, too dominant. Julian was nervous. And Angela—" Claire broke off, searching. "Angela looked at us strangely. At Julian. At me. Different. I can't explain it."

Olivia tilted her head. "You've been noticing power everywhere lately with Julian, Amanda, and now Richard. Do you think you're imagining patterns, or are you finally seeing what was always there?"

Claire pressed her lips together. "I don't know."

"That's all right," Olivia said evenly. "You don't need an answer today. But I want you to hold on to this: sometimes what looks like independence, or even rejection, is performance. An act meant to provoke you. Watch closely, Claire. Don't take everything at face value."

The word lodged in Claire's mind, sharp and persistent. Later, when she sat in her car, she heard it again: Performance. Julian's sudden farewell, his vanishing act, the replaced photograph, all replayed in a different light. Too abrupt. Too pointed. And if it was performance... then who was the audience? Claire felt that it was all too much. She needed a distraction.

After a sleepless night with Olivia's question echoing in her head — Who do you want to be, Claire? — she filled her Friday calendar with fabricated meetings, slipped a small suitcase into her trunk, and drove straight to the airport. The first available flight to Portland became her escape.

On the plane, doubt and desire argued inside her like lawyers. One voice hissed that it was reckless, even pathetic. The other whispered that this was her chance to stop analyzing and actually step into the thing she had only circled in thought. Julian had vanished. Her old life was splintered. If not now, when? She was almost fifty. She didn't want to die, never knowing who she might have been.

In her purse, the golden leash waited. Tonight, it would either mean nothing or it would answer everything.

Chapter 8

Amanda nearly stumbled when the text came through. She had almost given up hope. And now Claire was in Portland, not weeks from now but today. Six o'clock. Ritz-Carlton. Collar. It didn't read like an invitation. It was a summons.

Amanda dropped everything, drove home, and prepared with the kind of focus most people save for a high-stakes meeting. The choice of dress, the small rituals of grooming, even the act of locking the collar at her throat — they were her own way of breathing herself back into the world she longed for.

***

Claire, meanwhile, stood in a sex shop with the same tight, guilty sensation she used to feel when sneaking cigarettes in high school. Rows of leather and silicon surrounded her. She hated how clumsy she felt asking questions, how the young clerk's smirk suggested he'd seen a hundred nervous women like her. But she stayed. She studied, asked, chose. By the time she left with a discreetly wrapped package, her cheeks burned, but her pulse carried a strange pride. She was crossing a line, thrilling and perilous in equal measure.

If anyone had ever told her she'd be doing this, she would have laughed in their face and called it the most absurd joke imaginable. Yet here she was, slipping back into her hotel room like a thief, tearing open the package, learning the mechanics of what fastened where, how each piece should fit, what purpose it served. She even Googled to be sure.

The knock came at six sharp. Claire opened the door to Amanda, who, without hesitation, lowered herself to her knees, the collar already in place. It was a gesture so stark, so absolute, that Claire's hand tightened around the leash. For a moment, she almost laughed at herself, at the absurdity, at how unreal it looked. But Amanda wasn't smiling. Her eyes stayed down, her body still, waiting.

Without a word, Claire clipped the chain and tugged her inside. What followed wasn't polished. Claire's voice caught at first. Her instructions sometimes contradicted themselves. She poured wine too quickly and forgot what she'd meant to say. But Amanda didn't falter. She followed. She adjusted. When Claire touched her, guided her, Amanda moved as if this were the most natural rhythm in the world. It wasn't perfect. It was raw, uneven, but it lit Claire's body like nothing had in years.

Later, over dinner, the power dynamic didn't vanish. Instead, it simply shifted into subtler shades. Claire ordered the food, chose the wine, and asked the questions. Amanda answered openly, not coy, not hidden. That was when Claire learned the truth: Amanda didn't just work in marketing. She owned the agency. She had investments, properties, and sufficient wealth to never have to work another day. She was bright, articulate, and very successful. And yet here she was, sitting across from Claire with her collar hidden under a silk scarf, waiting for the next instruction.

It was that contrast that puzzled Claire most. Not the sex. Not the leash. But the way Amanda carried invisible traces of someone else's hand, someone else's training: the faint pause before she spoke, the care in how she set her glass down, the way her language felt trimmed, as if once it had been policed. None of that had come from Claire.

Amanda was free, prosperous, and independent, yet part of her still lived by the rules she had not written herself.

Claire couldn't decide whether that made Amanda fragile or indestructible. But she knew one thing for sure: Amanda wasn't a blank canvas. She had a past that still breathed through her.

***

On the flight back home, Claire turned the questions over in her mind until she was sick of them. Who was she trying to become? A dominant? Maybe. The thrill was undeniable. But was it a role she could live with, day after day? Amanda clearly wanted a life shaped around it. Claire wasn't sure she did. For her, it felt like testing borders, not building a house inside them.

All her life with Julian, she had subconsciously craved to be taken, without realizing she was expecting it from a man who could never give it. Instead, she learned to receive, and the experience left her divided. On one hand, it was playful, even fun. On the other hand, it carried a quiet guilt: I take, but I don't give. So she provoked Antonio, daring him to take her, only to discover that even this wasn't her thrill. The long-nurtured fantasy collapsed. Now she tested her borders again. This time, she was the one who took, who guided, who decided for the first time in her life. She wanted to feel it, to learn it, to step into someone else's skin. And to her astonishment and her shame, it worked.

And then came the other question she dreaded, one she couldn't push aside: was she really involved with a woman? Was this a turn she hadn't seen coming? The answer that rose was almost worse than yes or no: Amanda wasn't about gender at all. She was about possession. About belonging. About the power drawn tight between two people like a wire that could sing or snap. Claire hated those words. And yet their meaning thrilled her.

Chapter 9

It was a Thursday night when Claire and Richard boarded the private jet from Atlanta back to Chicago. The day had been a triumph—a meeting with a smaller bank Richard had been eyeing for acquisition had gone better than either of them had dared hope. The board had approved the plan, and thanks to Claire's sharp reading of the reports, they had shaved 8% off the asking price. Richard was in a rare mood, buoyed by the prospect of saving at least twenty million.

Once they were in the air, champagne was poured into their flutes. Richard lifted his glass toward her. "To your absolutely piercing eye, Claire. No one else would have ever spotted that error. You did. You saved us a fortune."

She smiled, their glasses meeting with a light chime. "I was thinking," Richard said, leaning back, "when we finalize the acquisition, you could head all the branches outside the state."

The words landed like a jolt. All 21 branches. The rest of the country. That would make her the second-most powerful person in the entire organization, perhaps even the first, one day. And the pay... she was already clearing over a million a year, but this would push her to at least one and a half. Maybe more. She swallowed, pulse quickening. Richard's smile had the indulgent warmth of a father watching a favored child succeed. "By the way, Claire," Richard said, "the Board approved another deal this week and we're bringing in a major new shareholder. The COMO Group, a fintech company out of Italy. They're taking a twenty-five percent stake in the bank, which makes them our largest shareholder, with a VIP seat on the Board. And they are bringing in their exclusive new app products. Mind-blowing banking technology. "

"Wow," Claire replied. "That means more capital for growth… more opportunities for acquisitions."

"Exactly," Richard said with a satisfied smile. "Things are going very well."

He set his glass down, watching her over the rim for a moment too long. "We should celebrate this properly," he said at last. "Not tonight. Next weekend. My place. Angela will be there." "Just the three of us." A beat, and then a slow, theatrical pause. "Angela… after that dinner, she hasn't stopped talking about you." His laugh was low, suggestive. "I even get jealous sometimes."

Claire stilled, unsure where this was heading, but the direction felt dangerous. She managed a smile, though.

"So, Claire, how about next Friday night? Are you free?" Claire heard herself say, slowly, "Yes, sure. Okay. Sounds good. Thanks."

Richard smiled, "Great, then. Let's have more champagne." She blinked, glass in hand, the taste suddenly sharp in her mouth. On the drive from the airport, Claire couldn't shake the residue of Richard's gaze or the sour aftertaste of his invitation. Atlanta had been a triumph, every meeting executed flawlessly, but the glow of success was dimmed by what lay ahead. My place. You, Angela, and I, he had said. The words clung to her like oil. Claire gripped the wheel a little tighter and shivered.

***

Richard arrived home in a triumphant mood. Angela loved those moments. She always saved her requests, her pushes, her quiet schemes for when Richard was riding high, when all he needed was the finishing touch of an elegant victory lap before giving her anything she wanted.

This time, she improvised. She met him at the door, framed by her own massive portrait on the wall. She kissed him hard, whispered that she had missed him, then sank to her knees. While she worked with just enough devotion not to outshine herself, Richard stood perfectly still, eyes drifting to the portrait, giving himself a silent high five for marrying such a beautiful, wise woman.

Later, after the shower, they stretched out by the indoor pool with champagne flutes in hand, the artificial light glinting across the still water.

"So," Angela said smoothly, "dinner again next Friday?"

"Yep." Richard's smile was relaxed, almost boyish. "She's an important wheel in my bank, Angie. And a new shareholder is coming in, so I need all my devoted people sticking together."

Angela tilted her head, studying him. Her silence pressed the question before her words did.

"I mentioned the new possible role," he continued. "After the acquisition, she could run all the branches outside the state. That's a serious rise. She'll take the bait."

Angela's lips curved. "Smart." She sipped, then let her voice drift out lightly, almost lazily. "So we want to keep her close. Loyal."

"That's correct," he said without hesitation.

Angela's eyes held his for a beat too long. "Then why," she asked playfully, "did you do that to her husband?"

Richard's smile deepened. He raised his glass, the gesture elegant but edged with something darker. "That," he said, savoring the pause, "was a moment of strength. Or weakness. I always aim to please you, don't I?"

Angela let his words hover in the air, not bothering to answer. Then, with a small, knowing smile, she leaned back against the cushions. "Well," she said lightly, as if brushing dust from her shoulder, "now that you're in such a generous mood... how about that red Porsche I love?

Chapter 10

Julian couldn't afford a luxury escape. Jetting off somewhere warm and throwing himself into azure waters was out of the question. Instead, he chose a run-down roadside motel, a stack of books, and his iPad. He hated every minute of it, but that was the point. Let Claire start looking for him. Let her sweat. Let her wonder where he was, who he was with, what he was doing. He knew her rhythms. She despised losing her grip on anything, especially him. Ten or twelve days of silence should do it. By then, when he decided to answer her texts, she'd be ready to summon him.

The coffee was awful, burnt, thin, and metallic. He took a sip anyway. It reminded him of his early days, long before Claire upgraded his tastes. Back when cheap, bitter coffee was routine. Back when he first saw her. And it wasn't at the photography event, as he'd always let her believe. No, the first time was about a month earlier, when he'd stumbled into a university alumni gathering for Business Management graduates from the last five years. He was there trolling for work, looking for someone who might want portraits, group photos, or whatnot. He only knew one person there,

Gordon, an acquaintance who'd graduated alongside Claire.

Julian had been sitting on a campus bench when he saw her talking to another woman, framed in a shaft of light, animated, alive. The most photogenic person he had ever seen. He couldn't look away.

Gordon caught him staring.

"What? That girl?" He smirked. Julian just nodded. "You know who that is?" Julian shook his head. "That's Claire Winters. Smartest and most beautiful in our year. Tough as hell, too." He laughed, then leaned in. "You know what she did to the most popular guy on campus?"
"What?" Julian asked, already half-dreading the answer.
"Ronnie. Top athlete, lady-killer. He tried to date her, and she said no. He got humiliated. At a party, out of spite, he announced she was the last virgin at the uni. She punched him in the nose so hard he disappeared for two weeks."

Gordon laughed again, then gave Julian a sideways look. "So, hey... drop it. Look at you, you're a loser with a fricking camera, man." And she scored a hell of a contract with a bank, by the way. I'd say she's making two hundred a year. And you what? Twenty grand?"

Julian swallowed his pride and said nothing. But in that moment, he made himself a silent promise: he would have that girl. And her money.

He watched her. Learned her rhythms. Followed from a distance. And when he finally saw her again, this time at a photography exhibition of local talent, he snapped a few frames and, against his nature, found the courage to approach her.

Julian had the eye, the skill, the taste. His work was always good and sometimes even touched with something close to genius. The problem was never the art. It was about turning art into a business. That meant leaving his comfort zone, meeting people, asking for work, pushing for deals, and getting things done. None of that was him. Talented? Yes. Even visionary at times. But lazy as hell.

As the only child, he had retired parents who weren't wealthy but comfortable enough. His mother had inherited a small nest egg from her father and, having nothing else to spend it on, she fed Julian monthly portions, enough to smooth the edges of his life. He thanked her warmly, accepted gracefully, and kept it quiet. To the outside world, Julian lived entirely on photography, and he wanted to keep it that way.

When he showed Claire the photos with his humble smile and his soft voice, she was mesmerized. She loved them. His cheeks flushed, his speech faltered into a stutter, something he could summon almost on command. She felt for him, thanked him, and, seeing his shyness, suggested they meet for coffee the next day. He agreed with a simple, "I'd be happy to."

That's how it began—Julian as the modest, unassuming artist and Claire, already solid and established, making real money at the bank at just twenty-four. He never pushed. Instead, he'd send her a new photograph, just enough to spark a conversation and lure her out, but never be the one to extend the invitation outright. Julian knew how to play the long game: wait, nudge, let her think each step was her idea. Coffees, movies, and walks. It all worked every single time.

Then came the lake shot. A windy afternoon, her dress lifting, her hair caught mid-whirl, and he captured that impossible, once-in-a-lifetime frame. The photograph was genius. She screamed with delight, laughed, then kissed him. He kissed her back. That night, they had sex, disastrous on his part, but she didn't mind. He was an artist. And artists, she thought, were like that, distracted, elegant, a little untamed.

A few months later, when he moved into her rental, Julian played his first real game. His uncle, a retired photographer, had gifted him all his equipment before disappearing to a Florida condo to finish out his life in peace. On the day Julian moved in, Claire was at work. He unpacked, cleaned the place until it gleamed, cooked an exquisite dinner, and chilled two expensive bottles of wine, courtesy of the regular deposits from his mother. A bouquet of fresh flowers waited on the table. When Claire walked in, it all looked like a dream, like paradise. She had found a man who adored her, and that much was obvious. Except for one small detail that she missed.

During dinner, after toasting her and thanking her, Julian slipped in a note of melancholy. Today, he said, was an important day for him professionally. He had invested all his savings into new equipment for a future studio. But it made him sad.

"Sad? That's crazy," she laughed. "It's amazing!"

"Sad," he repeated softly, "because I had a deal lined up before we decided to live together, and now…I'm afraid I won't be able to help you with rent for a few months."

She waved it off. "Oh, that's nothing."

He thanked her again. And when the second bottle of wine was nearly gone, he cemented his strategy with precision. He lowered himself gracefully in front of her, eyes locked on hers, and kissed her leg just above the knee. Then another kiss, higher this time, slow, thoughtful. She giggled, eased back, the tension leaving her shoulders. When his tongue finally found her, she closed her eyes, smiling, feeling elevated, worshiped, and happy.

Dinners followed, each one more elaborate than the last. His mother's monthly allowance barely covered the ingredients for the French and Italian recipes he had mastered, but he made sure Claire was living in a dream. The apartment was always spotless, with dinner waiting and wine poured. When she came home drained from long hours at the bank, his hands would find her shoulders, kneading away the day.

Bit by bit, he conditioned her into believing her pleasure mattered more than his. Almost every night, and most mornings too, he went down on her until it became less a treat and more an accepted routine.

Sometimes he worked, of course, but his earnings barely covered their wine bill. His mother's money filled in the rest. Then, one weekend, he took her back to the lake, the exact same spot where he had captured that unforgettable photograph. There, he unrolled a life-sized print of it, dropped to one knee, and proposed. Claire said yes.

**

There was one dinner Julian would remember for a long time. He was proud of how well he played it. It was only a few months after the wedding, just days after Claire received her first promotion at the bank. They were dining on tuna steaks with arugula salad and a chilled bottle of Chardonnay when Julian put on his best "troubled" face. He didn't speak at first, letting the silence hang until she finally asked, near the end of the meal:

"Bad day, honey?"

"Oh, no," he sighed, "not really. Just… this meeting with a friend this morning. It's still bothering me."

"What happened?" she pressed, eager to draw it out.

Julian leaned back, exhaling as though reluctant. "He's in the photography world too, connected with those big ad agencies, huge networks. I asked if he could help me get in, maybe score a freelance contract. Full-time, real work."

Claire nodded, sipping her wine. "And?"

"He said he could introduce me to the top management. But…" Julian paused, frowning just enough. "There's a stumbling block. I don't have a proper studio. They'd need a place for models, proper shoots. I can't exactly invite them to my mom's garage."

Claire tilted her head. "Julian, if you're serious about working with top agencies, that could mean big money. You need a studio."

He shook his head slowly, as though weighed down by responsibility. "I know, but I can't even afford rent right now. I'm still paying off the equipment. It's too much."

"Julian," she cut him off, firm but glowing with determination, "we're family now. We'll do it properly. I'll help with the rent."

Her eyes shone with belief, with hope for his success. He tensed, giving her the picture of reluctance, then let it soften into a grateful smile. Just enough hesitation, just enough performance.

"You're the best, Claire. You're taking me forward. You're my captain." He laughed lightly, adding with just the right note of charm, "And as all good captains do, you can order me to serve you."

She laughed, pleased, and motioned across the table. "Then start by cleaning this up and coming to the sofa." She winked, lifting her glass as she reached for the remote. Julian jumped to obey. Three weeks later, his equipment was moved into a proper studio with Claire's name on the lease.

Slowly, almost imperceptibly, Julian steered Claire into becoming the boss of the family. Initially, she made decisions after consulting with him. Later, she stopped mentioning them altogether. Vacations were booked, and major purchases were always settled by her hand. What she never recognized was how expertly Julian had nudged her into that role, how each choice she thought was hers alone had been quietly guided.

In the small, daily details, he surrendered. Gradually, Claire forgot how to cook, how to clean, how to manage laundry. She worked. He served. And yet his service came at a cost, subtle, invisible, manipulative. By the time his studio was set up and some business began to flow, it seemed effortless, as though it had simply happened. Compared to Claire's earnings, it was nothing, but at least it freed him from depending entirely on his mother's quiet deposits, which, of course, never stopped. For

Julian, it meant a bit more money in his pocket and more freedom to maneuver.

Then Claire became pregnant, and when Chloe was born, Julian immediately offered, no, insisted, that he would stay with the baby so Claire could return to work as soon as possible. He certainly loved his daughter, but even she, inevitably, became part of his strategy. Another lever to shape his life in precisely the way that suited him best.

***

The first real crack in their marriage showed itself during a vacation in Mexico. Chloe was four. She was old enough to travel easily, and Claire thought a week away would do them all good. Claire would never know the real story behind the trip. Initially, she had wanted Jamaica. She'd found a beautiful resort, researched everything, and shown Julian. He'd glanced at it with little enthusiasm and said, "If that's what you wish, sure, baby." She nodded, already planning to book it that week.

The next evening, or maybe the one after, she came home late. Chloe was already asleep. Claire tiptoed into her daughter's room, tucked the blanket around her, and kissed her forehead. Then she noticed a drawing on the little table, crayons scattered everywhere.

It was simple but striking—sun, sea, a crooked palm tree. And underneath, in uneven letters, it read: *Mexic*. The *o* was missing. Claire smiled, lifted the paper, and studied it. She put it back before leaving the room.

Later, over dinner and their customary glasses of wine, she said, "Julian, would you be super mad if I changed our plans and we went to Mexico instead of Jamaica?"

He looked at her, surprised. Breathed out. Paused. Took a sip of wine. Then said, "You change plans so quickly, Claire... but again—who's the boss?" He smiled. "Wherever the boss wants to go, I'll follow. That's my job." His tone was pure devotion, polished servitude. Then he added, softer, "All I care about is the taste of ocean salt on your skin."

"Wow," she laughed. "That's sexy. And since our trip is in two weeks, maybe you should start rehearsing now."

He set down his glass, slid his hands over her hips, and whispered, "With pleasure." She closed her eyes and pictured the beach.

What she didn't know was what had happened earlier that day. When Julian first heard "Jamaica," his stomach turned. He had been there once as a child, and for reasons buried and half-forgotten, the place unsettled him still. He couldn't bring himself to go back. But he wouldn't tell Claire that. Not directly. Instead, he opened his laptop, googled "how would a four-year-old draw sun, beach, sea." He studied the images carefully. Then he copied one. Handed it to Chloe. Asked her to color it however she liked. Finally, he told her to copy a word onto the page. She did. He told her it was the name of a beach. He knew Claire would see it. He knew she'd act.

***

On the plane, they met another couple, Sam and Susan, about the same age as Claire and Julian. Coincidentally, they were staying at the same hotel.

The four of them fell into an easy rhythm: beach during the day, bars and restaurants at night. Except, most of the time, it was really three of them—Claire, Sam, and Susan. Julian always had a reason to stay behind. Chloe needed to nap, to eat, to avoid the sun. He was happy to put her to bed early and settle in with a book, a show, or his iPad. He never wanted the noise of the bars, the energy of the restaurants, the unexpected messiness of vacationing. Everything with Julian was always structured, always planned, and somehow always arranged around his own comfort.

But that wasn't the real issue. The real issue revealed itself one evening. They had a reservation for four, plus Chloe. Claire and Julian arrived on time and were seated. A minute later, she spotted Sam and Susan entering the restaurant, but then... they vanished. Ten minutes or so after they reappeared, apologizing, laughing, a little disheveled. Susan's hair wasn't quite in place. Claire said nothing, but she noticed.

Later, after dinner, Julian went back to the hotel room with Chloe while Claire followed Sam and Susan to the bar. As Sam stepped away to order drinks, Susan leaned in close, giggling, her voice lowered to a conspiratorial whisper. She confessed that they had, in fact, arrived at the restaurant on time, but at the last second, Sam had pulled her into the washroom for a quickie. "Imagine that, Claire!" she laughed, wine glinting in her eyes. "He just pinned me against the wall and—" She broke off in another fit of giggles. "God, I think I left my underwear in there."

Claire froze. It wasn't the act itself that shocked her. It was the idea. The moment. The audacity. The raw hunger of it. A man who couldn't wait. A woman who let herself be taken. She had never experienced anything like that in her life. And the more Susan talked, the more Claire felt an ache, a gnawing sense of having been cheated out of some primal, electric truth of living. Back in the hotel room, she told Julian. He barely looked up, only shrugged. "Stupid," he said flatly.

"You think so?" Claire's voice sharpened. Her chest was tight, her face hot. "You never do anything on impulse. You never want me right here, right now. That's what I'd like, Julian. That's what I want."

He looked at her then, his eyes wide, but empty, almost disbelieving.

"But you get everything you want," he murmured. "Anything you ask for…"

"Do I?" she hissed. "How about being a man for once and showing it? How about wanting me without permission, without planning? How about doing something crazy?"

The silence between them grew heavy. Claire's pulse hammered with both fury and shame. Why did she have to ask for this? Why did she have to beg? Julian said nothing. Inside, his thoughts twisted, dark and sharp. Words formed that he knew he could never speak. If Claire had heard them, if she had glimpsed even a corner of what really went through his mind, she would not have recognized the man in front of her. And she would have been terrified. Instead, silence stretched between them, heavy and bitter. That fight ruined the trip. They wouldn't take another vacation together for six years.

Chapter 11

A few years ago, one late October evening, Julian noticed Claire's passport lying on the floor near her shoes, half-spilled from the handbag she'd abandoned in a rush. The bag was on its side; the passport must have slipped out. He picked it up, walked quietly into the garage, unlocked her car, and slid it between the driver's seat and the center console—the black hole where keys, rings, licenses, and other things vanished for days. He knew Claire was flying to London the next morning with Richard and a few other bank executives. It was an important trip, one she'd never make without him now. Not unless Julian allowed it. Smiling to himself, he went to bed.

Morning broke into chaos. Claire was frantic; her passport was gone. She swore it had been in her bag the night before, swore she had taken it to the office to fill out forms, and then brought it back. Julian scratched his head, played confused. He told her she was always so messy, constantly losing things, but he tried to help. She tore through the house in panic. Without that passport, London was finished. Worse, Richard, who was counting on her, might fire her for it. She was shaking, near collapse, when Julian stopped in the middle of the living room. Then, turning to her, "Wait. What did you do last night?"

"Nothing. I came home, dropped my bag right there, and went upstairs."

He nodded gravely. "Right. You came home. Then..." His eyes lit up. "The car!"

He hurried into the garage with Claire at his heels, searching carefully until, with a triumphant shout, he pulled it free. "There it is!"

"Oh my God, I'm saved!" she screamed, throwing her arms around him, kissing him with relief. "Thank you, Julian! Thank you so much! But how?... I mean, I swear I left it in my bag."

He hugged her calmly, smiling, almost tenderly. "Claire, you're exhausted. You probably dropped it in the car without realizing. But you're welcome. I'm here for you. Always," he said simply, before stepping back into the house. She rushed to gather her things, kissed him and Chloe goodbye at the door, and ran for the car. He called after her: "Oh, one tiny thing. Can I send you a link? A lens I've had my eye on. Ten percent cheaper in London."

"Of course," she beamed, radiant with gratitude. "Anything, my savior!" She waved. Julian took

Chloe's hand and, as they both stood there watching Claire drive away, he congratulated himself on a flawless performance and a new expensive lens.

Chloe, eight at the time, swung his hand as they walked inside the house, speaking almost like she was telling a secret. "Dad, I saw Mom's passport on the floor last night. Next to her bag. How did it end up in her car?"

Julian froze for a split second. That was an unexpected witness. He forced a gentle smile. "You might've seen something else, sweetheart. Lots of things fall out of Mom's purse."

Chloe's head tilted stubbornly. "No. I'm sure it was her passport." Then, with the carelessness only children have, she shrugged. Julian's pulse kicked up. He squeezed her hand, shifting quickly. "How about a movie today? Just you and me."

Her face lit up. "Yay!" She skipped beside him, her question forgotten at least for now. But Julian knew questions like that never vanished. They just went quiet. And sometimes, years later, they came back.

***

The sticky motel soured his mood. But money mattered now. Their separation had been strange. Claire left, yet she never raised a single question about expenses. She still paid his studio rent and still covered the house utilities. She simply didn't live there anymore. Whatever Julian made from photography, he kept for himself, which wasn't much. He lived modestly. His idea of luxury was simple: a spotless house, silence, and himself on the sofa with the TV glowing. A book or an online game to pass the hours. That was enough. The best days were the ones that demanded nothing of him. No better, no worse, just the same. That sameness suited him. All he needed was someone to sponsor his comfort.

Now he was stuck in a grimy motel. Claire had sent four texts, and he hadn't replied. He switched off Read receipts so she'd only see Delivered. She called once. He let it ring. Let her suffer. Let her stew over what she'd done to him.

There was little else to do. He emailed the studio landlord to say he'd be leaving in sixty days. After his little hideout here, he'd go pack up, haul some things to his mother's garage, and some back to the house. Divorce hadn't been discussed, and Julian hoped it wouldn't be. He was banking on the game.

Claire would summon him back. She had to. There is no other way, he told himself. Think positive, Julian. Two or three more days here, then he'd reply. A casual text. Sorry, been busy, away. He'd play dumb. Play the man who had already moved on.

***

Claire drove back from the office, the late Monday sun sliding low across the streets. Her session with Olivia wasn't until five, still an hour to spare. At first, she thought of heading to her apartment, taking a shower, and changing. But another thought intruded. Julian. She wasn't far from his studio. Maybe it was worth checking on him again. Almost without deciding, she turned, drove a few blocks, and found a parking spot. The studio sat across the street, its windows dark, the sign flipped to Closed. He wasn't there.

Claire lingered in the car, debating. Drive away, keep her distance, or check inside? She had the keys. Reluctantly, she got out, crossed the street, and let herself in.

The air was stale, heavy. He hadn't been there for days. The last time she'd seen him was that strange doorstep performance, his little speech about moving on. She scanned the room. Nothing had changed since her last visit. Her photo, once looming like a shrine, was now replaced by that bleak industrial landscape. This time, she felt nothing about it. Not anger, not even loss. Just emptiness. Who were you kidding, Julian? she thought as she moved toward the washroom.

On the way out, she noticed the storage door. It was ajar. Odd. Julian had always kept it locked. Was it like this the last time? Had she missed it? She pushed it open. The cramped space smelled of dust and cardboard. Shelves sagged with boxes, binders, old scraps of a life. She pulled one open. It had photographs and magazine cutouts. Another had bank statements, neatly sorted, labeled by year.

She flipped through a folder absentmindedly, half from nostalgia. Oh, that year. The one when they moved in together. When they got married. Back when the future felt infinite. Sinking into a chair, she leafed through the pages. Numbers, deposits, dull print. Until one line caught her eye.

Maureen Collins, deposit $2,000. June 28th.

She frowned. His mother. She turned the page. Maureen Collins, deposit $2,000. July 28th. Then August. September. October. Every single month. Claire froze. She had never known.

He had never told her. All those years, he had insisted his photography kept him afloat. That he had been paying off the equipment he had invested in. She rifled faster through the statements. No equipment payoff. No large transfers. No evidence of income from photography at all. No cash withdrawals either. Nothing. Her stomach tightened. She thought for a moment and then lifted the box of statements and walked out, the studio door clicking shut behind her. At home, she would comb through them page by page. Something in her head warned her that what lay inside was not bookkeeping, but revelation.

Later that day, Claire opened Julian's box again. She retrieved the neatly labeled folders, year after year, month by month, and plunged into the dry, lifeless terrain of transactions. She combed through each line, fishing for patterns, for clues, for the faintest outline of the secret life Julian might have been living. By evening, determined to dig deeper, Claire picked up the phone. She called the widow of Julian's late uncle, the same uncle who had supposedly sold him the photography studio equipment. The truth came out harsh and ugly: He hadn't bought it. It had been a gift. He had lied. About the debt, about why he couldn't share rent payments in those first years with her, and about contracts with ad agencies that never happened. He had maneuvered her into covering his studio rent, year after year. Claire hung up and stared at the folder as if it might argue back. A lie was on every single page.

Chapter 12

Friday morning, the very Friday of Richard's looming dinner, Claire drove past the studio once more and returned the box with bank statements to its shelf. She closed the storage door, lingered a moment, and glanced around. Julian still hadn't appeared. Where was he? A picture rose in her mind: Julian somewhere in a hotel by the sea, or in the mountains, his face buried between another woman's thighs, working himself to exhaustion with that diligent tongue of his. Claire smirked. He was far from perfect. She knew it now.

No, the truth with Julian was almost certainly darker and smaller. A life reduced to lying, hiding, scheming, surviving. But then… she had just learned he was capable of surprising her, and that uncertainty was the cruelest thing of all. She might never really know the truth.

She locked the studio and left, her mind already pivoting toward her plans for today— first Olivia, then the office, then the dinner waiting like a masked trap at the end of the day. A dangerous evening, dressed in civility. When she slipped back into her car, something warm and treacherously sweet coiled low inside her. It was the pull of the evening ahead with the candles, the wine, with

Richard's voice wrapping around her, and Angela's hungry eyes watching too closely. Not lust alone, but the sense of stepping into a current she might not control. She couldn't name it, only that it thrilled her as much as it unnerved her. And she no longer trusted herself to resist.

***

Claire sat forward, her face calm, concentrated, almost emotionless. "It was all a lie, Olivia. The studio equipment, the rent, and the ad contracts — none of it was true. His mother was wiring him money every month, and he let me carry the rest. His uncle had gifted the equipment, and he told me he had been paying it off for months. Or years."

Olivia studied her for a second, then said, "And what's the part that unsettles you most, the money or the deception?"

"The deception," Claire answered without hesitation. "I thought we were partners. I thought I was supporting him because he was building something, trying. In reality, I was propping up… nothing. Or worse… a performance."

Olivia nodded. "So the question isn't whether he failed as a provider. It's whether he manipulated you into playing a role you never agreed to."

Claire's throat tightened. "That's exactly it. Like I've been living in a system he designed, and I never saw it. And the worst part is, I can't tell if I'm inventing that to explain it, or if it's the truth."

"That's the tension," Olivia said softly. "Between what you know, the lies you can prove, and what you feel that the whole marriage may have been orchestrated. People often protect themselves with softer explanations. But your unease is telling you something. It's not noise. It's data."

Claire lifted her eyes. "So what do I do with it?"

Olivia leaned back. "You sit with it until you know whether it's suspicion or recognition. That difference matters more than action right now."

Claire breathed out. "I don't know which it is yet. But if it's recognition, if I've really been living like this... then I need to know it for sure... From him."

Olivia gave the faintest nod. "That sounds like your truth is finally taking shape." Then she glanced at the clock and back at Claire. "And what about tonight? How do you feel about the dinner?"

Claire hesitated. "Strange. Restless." She searched for the word. "Excited, even. But not in a safe way."

"What do you expect from it?"

"A show, maybe. A performance. Richard is never just Richard. Angela's the same." Claire's lips pressed together. "I can't shake the feeling this isn't only about food and wine, and a social evening. My radar tells me there's something staged, something waiting to happen."

Olivia tilted her head. "And your worst fears?"

Claire exhaled through her nose. "That's the problem. I can't name them. It's more like... standing at the edge of a current and knowing it could pull me under. Part of me thinks they're predators, in their own polished way. But maybe I'm imagining it."

"Maybe," Olivia said evenly. "Or maybe your body is reading what your mind hasn't yet formed into words."

Claire looked down at her hands. "Either way, I want to see where it leads."

***

Claire's choice for the evening was a tiny, elegant black dress, simple, lethal, sexy as hell. She had given it serious thought before stepping into it.

Why provoke? Why invite? Her feelings were tangled. Richard's eyes on the plane had meant far more than a dinner invitation, and she knew it. She felt it. Was she going to surrender to his claim or theirs? No. She was certain of that. But she wanted to walk the edge, test the air, discover how far he or both of them were willing to go, and why.

What was the agenda? Political leverage? A sexual game? Or nothing at all? Maybe it was just her imagination running riot after Amanda, after Jamaica, after Portland. These days, she saw sexual tension everywhere, even in shadows. Maybe Richard was nothing more than Richard. Wrong or not, she knew one thing: tonight, she looked devastating. She snapped a selfie and sent it to Amanda. Before she'd even chosen her lipstick, the reply came: *You are gorgeous.* Claire smiled. I am, she thought.

The taxi ride felt suspended in anticipation. No point in driving herself, she knew there wouldn't be a drop of sobriety expected at Richard's table. As the car turned into his long driveway, she saw him outside, standing by a sleek black Mercedes, engaged in conversation with another man. Bad timing. To get out now meant interrupting. But there was no other choice.

Richard, facing her, noticed the car approach. He raised a hand, half-wave, half-wait. The man beside him didn't even turn. Claire stepped out, heels clicking on the stone. For a moment, she froze, torn between walking toward Richard or simply slipping inside the house. The taxi pulled away, leaving her exposed. Richard's attention broke. He said something to the man, then gestured toward her. The stranger turned. And Claire's heart sank, her stomach dropped, her face flushed. What? Antonio? How the hell was that even possible?

He froze too, just for a beat, before his expression shifted from polite neutrality to stunned recognition, to something like awe. His voice trembled as he said, "Claire?"

Richard stopped dead, as though struck by lightning. The mask slipped from his face, raw surprise cutting through.

Claire forced civility, literally pushing her lips into a smile. "Hi, Antonio."

Antonio stepped forward instinctively, closing the space between them, his hands catching her elbows as if to anchor himself in the reality of her presence. "God, Claire…It's been a while…" His voice cracked on her name.

Richard's gaze snapped between them, trying to decode all of it. He had seen the shock, the recognition, and noted the intimacy that needed no words.

"You two know each other?" Richard finally asked, his tone deceptively casual, though his eyes probed, sharp and calculating.

Antonio turned to him, his face open, bright, a strange mix of delight and surprise. "We do," he said simply. Then, after a pause, his smile widened. "Claire has been a friend of my sister's for a while." A beat. His eyes flicked to Claire's, steady, charged. "And... to be honest, Richard, I fell for her the moment we met. But she never said yes."

Claire held his gaze, caught. The first part of the sentence sounded like a confession. He fell for her... But in their shared twisted reality, so had she. The second part, where she had never said yes, probably meant the breakfast she had missed... Her mind spun, but still, she felt it right there—that same pull she had felt in Jamaica, pressed against that wall that failed her then but seemed alive now. A sudden wave of arousal flooded her, sharp and unwelcome, but delicious. Her body betrayed her instantly. And her lingerie whispered the truth with that damp, silky sensation. His hands still on her arms, his eyes carrying both relief and regret—

relief that she stood before him again, and regret for the way their first encounter had ended — ignited something in her. She managed a smile, playing along, her voice even. "Old days, Antonio. Old days..."

"Wow," Richard cut in, his attempt at enthusiasm failed to mask the unease threading his voice. "Antonio is our new shareholder, Claire. The COMO Group."

Claire blinked. What? Of all possibilities, this coincidence felt like fate's fricking trick. She didn't answer, just watched Richard's face as the realization hit.

His composure slipped, bewilderment first, then the raw recognition that he had lost ground. More than ground... he had lost the game entirely. The owner of the COMO Group, his bank's largest new shareholder, had just declared himself involved with Claire Winters, his own Vice President of Operations. Holy fuck. And yes, the image of Claire between him and Angela in bed vanished, melting into nothingness. Richard could almost hear the dominoes falling, and Claire slipping through his fingers. And, though she wasn't yet aware, Angela's too. "Well," Richard said at last, his voice steadier than his face, "since that's the case... may I offer you dinner, Antonio? I invited Claire to celebrate the deal in Atlanta. She was the one who shaved over twenty million off the asking price. The least we can do is raise a glass to her."

Antonio turned to him smoothly, nodding. "Gladly, Richard. You've given me the chance to see an old... friend again. I had no idea Claire worked at the bank. She never shared the details."

Claire said nothing, only smiled. But inside, she marveled. Antonio had lied for her with such elegance, crafting a perfect story in a heartbeat. He had shielded her, claimed her, and in doing so had lifted her clean out of Richard's grasp. That was dominance at its most subtle, undeniable. She could tell that by how Richard walked through that front door. By how his shoulders sagged, by how he didn't even glance at the portrait of Angela...

Antonio and Claire followed. He was still holding her hand. She didn't even notice. It felt inevitable, as if it had always been that way.

***

Angela couldn't mask her surprise when Antonio walked back in with Claire at his side. She hadn't counted on that. The arrangement with Richard had been clear: Claire, alone. Easy prey. Angela had plans for her—carefully drawn, deliciously detailed. And now? What the fuck was happening? Antonio wasn't simply staying for dinner. He was practically glued to Claire, as if they'd known each other for years.

The first moment she got close enough to Richard, and out of earshot, she hissed, "What the fuck, Richard?"

"Hush," he warned, flashing her a glance sharp enough to cut. Then, lowering his voice, "Imagine they're old friends... Who knew? Worse, babe, he's clearly invested in her. I mean... You know.."

Angela's eyes narrowed. That changed everything. The entire dynamic flipped in an instant. Even Richard couldn't ignore it: Antonio and his money were the keystone of the bank's future and of Richard's fat, happy retirement. Angela knew it. Which meant her little scheme would have to be folded, rolled tight, and shoved, well, exactly where she was picturing as she glared across the kitchen at Richard's ass. He was the one to blame for this disaster. Even if he never saw it coming.

At the table, the conversation flowed easily enough. Richard played the most adorable host, Angela forced her smile and contributed when she had to, though her mind was elsewhere—schemes, shifting dynamics, and a future that seemed to twist tighter with every glass of wine. She barely tasted the food.

The conversation centered on the latest merger, specifically how Claire had identified a beneficial reporting error.

"By the way, Richard, dinner is a fantastic idea," Antonio said smoothly. "But I believe you also signed off on a fat bonus for Claire, didn't you?"

Richard's smile flickered. For a fraction of a second, the mask slipped. A bonus was never part of his plan. Quite the opposite. But now, cornered, there was no graceful way out.

"You've ruined my Monday's surprise, Antonio."

Antonio leaned back, feigning innocence. "Ah, my bad. I thought Claire already knew. But since I spoiled it, why not tell her now?"

Claire hid her astonishment behind her wineglass. She knew precisely what Antonio was doing—pinning Richard down, forcing his hand, making sure she left the table with more than polite compliments.

She slipped on her most gracious mask. "There's nothing I did that deserved a bonus. I only did my job."

"And you did it exceptionally well," Antonio interjected, his eyes lingering on her a moment too long.

Richard's jaw flexed before his smile widened again, his mind cursing. Fuck you, Antonio. You walked in five minutes ago, and you're already spending my money. Out loud, he declared with easy grandeur:

"Yes, Claire. A one-time bonus. Half a million. Payable by the end of the month."

Claire inclined her head in acknowledgment, careful, conscious. "Thank you, boss." She used the word boss on purpose. It was a balm for Richard's pride, though she knew Antonio had already landed the deeper cut. And the night was only beginning.

***

Antonio offered to drive Claire home. Of course he did. Richard and Angela walked them to the car, their farewells warm, perfectly social. On the surface, the dinner had been a success. Beneath it, everyone, except Antonio, perhaps, was eager to see it end. As the Mercedes disappeared down the long driveway, Richard's smile evaporated. His face hardened, eyes turning cold and calculating. He exhaled through his nose, then muttered, "That was an unexpected and very unfortunate development."

Angela's lips curved faintly, but she said nothing. Her mind was already working on what she could extract from him for a failure he couldn't possibly have prevented. Of course, he hadn't known. How could he have guessed that Antonio and Claire were connected? Pure accident. But did she care? Not at all. An accident was still leverage, and leverage was power. As they went inside, Richard's hand slid possessively down to Angela's perfect ass. She glanced sideways, her voice cool, flat: "Not tonight." His fingers froze, then withdrew, reluctant but obedient. The message was clear. Not tonight.

***

Claire's body trembled. Being alone in the car with Antonio dragged her straight back to Jamaica—the busted lip, the faked orgasm, the bitter monologue in the mirror. She wasn't sure she wanted to be here now. And yet, here she was.

Antonio looked composed, but his eyes betrayed him. They were tender, sincere, glancing at her over and over, as though searching for words he couldn't quite summon. Finally, he found them.

"I'm truly sorry for what happened in Jamaica, Claire. I never meant for it to go that way." She gave the smallest nod, holding her silence.

He hesitated, then pushed on, his voice low, unguarded. "When I saw you at the restaurant, I was floored. You looked... well, you still do, you look like a dream come true. Like the woman I've been searching for all my life. The fantasy that feels too perfect to exist. And then, when we met on the courts, I—"

She cut him off gently. "It wasn't your fault, Antonio. It was my stupid game. I wrote the rules. You just played along."

He swallowed hard. She noticed his hands falter slightly on the wheel. There was a beat of silence before he breathed out, almost as if exhaling courage. "Would you have dinner with me tomorrow? I'd love the chance to fix this, Claire." The directness of it, the honesty, took her aback. She wasn't ready. Not with everything piling up—Julian's lies, Amanda's body still ghosting her skin, Richard and Angela circling like wolves. And now

Antonio. It was too much. The car rolled to a stop outside her building. She turned toward him. "Dinner... okay," she murmured. His eyes lit, sharp and boyish at once. "Tomorrow, here. Seven o'clock. Deal?" She only nodded. He stepped out and walked her to the door. As her hand touched the handle, his voice dropped to a whisper. "I can't tell you how happy I am that I've found you, Claire."

She looked at him, then opened the door without a word. No wave, no backward glance, only the straight line of her body moving toward the elevator. And then, inside, it hit her: she hadn't even said goodbye.

Chapter 13

Claire's morning began with a text from Julian.

Sorry for not coming back earlier. Was out of the country. Back now. Give me a call if still important.

She stared at it, the words staring back. It didn't sound like Julian. Not his style. Not his voice. There was a crispness, a trace of masculinity in it, something she had never once noticed in him. He had never written like that. What a change, she thought. Or was it? The bank statements surfaced in her mind. Maybe the message itself was just another piece of his game, another carefully constructed lie. A diversion. A mask.

She set the phone down without answering. She needed to think. The first shock of Julian's little performance on her doorstep had faded. Clarity replaced it, and with clarity came something sharper: the realization she no longer wanted him back. The desire to summon him, to straighten him out, to put him "back in his place" was gone. More unsettling still was the thought that slid in after: she didn't want him sexually anymore. Not after the lies. Not after the discovery of who he really was. She had no appetite for that head bowed between her legs, no craving for the old rhythm of his tongue. That, too, had died with the bank statements.

Claire made herself a cup of coffee and sat at the wide window overlooking the lake. Her heart tightened with a sensation she despised: the feeling that life was teetering on the edge of a shift. Complicated. Collapsing. Out of her control.

Why had she agreed to dinner tonight? That single "yes" had made everything worse. And Antonio, out of all the improbable scenarios, it had to be him. The man from Jamaica was now the bank's new largest shareholder. That meant proximity. That meant eyes on her. And it meant she would have to manage him carefully and walk away without leaving blood on the floor.

Her thoughts drifted to Amanda. To that Portland hotel. To the vision of Amanda's perfect body, open, eager, waiting. For one sharp second, Claire wanted to be there, standing behind her, commanding that sweet expectancy. She cursed under her breath, tried to shake the image off. What the hell was happening to her? Why did every road in her mind seem to end with sex? It puzzled her. All those years with Julian, she had never been haunted by such thoughts. She had known the script: she'd come home, they'd have dinner, and then he'd be there, eager to please, and it would always be up to her. If she weren't in the mood, she'd fake it. If she were, and the stars aligned with the rhythm of his tongue, she'd let it happen.

For years, he had never demanded his own pleasure. At some point, she'd forgotten he even had one. Sometimes, after a glass too many of wine, she'd tell him to take care of himself while she watched his hand move in a desperate attempt to follow her command. Once, though, drunk, she crossed the line. She extended her foot, nudged him forward, and said flatly: "Do it here." He obeyed, almost too quickly. And when it was over, she stared, frozen, unable to decide what came next. His whisper—"Can I clean it?"—shook her. Before she could answer, he was already following through, diligent, wordless. She remembered waking the next morning, seething at herself, angry for having made him do it. She didn't know how to behave after, what to say.

She hated the sting of shame when fragments of last night, always blurred by wine, crept back. She had never thought of herself as wanton, never the type to cross lines carelessly. Yet somehow, with a steady fog of drink, she found herself doing things that left her fighting morning guilt. What she didn't see was how patient, how deliberate Julian's method had been, guiding her step by step into a role she never chose.

Before she could decide what to do that morning, his head was already buried between her thighs again, as if nothing had happened. She closed her eyes, gave him a few minutes, and faked it.

Her thoughts slowly shifted to dinner with Antonio, and she made herself a promise: whatever the night brought, she would not let it end in his bed.

***

Julian had grown to love Saturdays. Claire used to reserve that day for Chloe, trying to make up for the hours her work consumed during the week, and Julian always retreated to his studio under the guise of being busiest on Saturdays. The truth was simpler: he just loved the silence. The luxury of procrastination. Doing nothing at all.

Sometimes, though, work did arrive. Like today. Almost as soon as he unlocked the studio, two women walked in. They were graceful, cheerful, and openly affectionate with each other. They wanted an anniversary shoot. Julian liked them instantly. Easy clients. They spent nearly two hours discussing clothes, timing, and locations. He quoted them $750 for a four-hour session; they agreed, left a deposit, and disappeared into the late morning.

When the door closed, Julian made himself a cup of tea. He wondered, almost in disbelief, how he could have forgotten to lock the storage, then let it go and scrolled blankly through the news. His mind, as always, circled back to Claire. He'd texted her last night. She hadn't replied. That was fine, he told himself. Give her another day. But what if she didn't respond at all? What then? He had no plan B. He never needed one. Plan A had always been enough. Claire was predictable. Or so he imagined.

The shrill ring of the studio phone jolted him. Think of the devil, he thought. Must be Claire. He picked up, forcing his voice into businesslike formality. "Julian's Photos. How can I help you?"

There was a pause. Then a voice came, low, velvety, laced with a tiny half-laugh. "Hi, Julian. This is Angela. Richard's wife. Remember me?"

Julian's stomach turned. Of all the voices in the world, not this one. Memories slammed into him. His eyes slid to the podium, to the neat arrangement of lights, to the vacant square of floor where months ago his life had twisted into something he'd never named aloud. His mouth filled with a salty tang.

"Yes," he managed, his voice raw. "Angela. I remember."

"Good," she replied, crisp and calm. "I need to see you. There's something we could both be interested in."

He swallowed that taste clinging to his throat. "When?" He asked and licked his dry lips.

"Monday morning," she said smoothly. And as if she could see him nod, she carried on, "Be at the studio by 9 am." The line went dead. Julian lowered the receiver slowly, his fingers trembling against the plastic. And then he felt it—an erection. The first in months.

Almost eight months earlier.

"Hey, Julian—" Claire's voice trailed from the hall as she slipped on her shoes. "I almost forgot. I told Richard yesterday you were a pro photographer, and he asked if you could do a photoshoot for his wife." Julian tensed. He was still in the kitchen, loading the dishwasher.

"I left his number on the counter," she called, already halfway out the door. "Call him. Don't let me down." She didn't wait for his reply. The door clicked shut behind her.

Julian walked over to the counter. Beside his wallet and phone lay a sticky note: a number and four words, "Richard, photoshoot. Must call." He stared at it. He didn't like this. No, he actually hated this. Being handed clients, being told what to do. Or did he, really? The truth, buried deep, was more complicated. He loved it, though he never admitted it, not even to himself. He dressed up the thrill as resentment, cloaking his hunger in irritation. In the marrow of his bones, he knew what those moments did to him whenever she gave any kind of instructions. But the ones whispered in bed… Oh, those were his purest intoxication.

Again and again, his mind returned to that night, to his own voice, "Can I clean it?" Even her half nod, or maybe even the absence of it—he wasn't sure if he had actually seen that nod— had sliced through him like a whip and crowned him at the same time. That was his summit, his Everest. He climbed it with perfect devotion. He remembered how happy he'd felt afterward, as though his years of subtle labor, nudging, prodding, sculpting her into what he needed her to be, had finally borne some fruit. Because that's what it was, wasn't it? He'd been polishing Claire from the very beginning, pushing her into a role she had only brushed against naturally. She had the hints of it, yes, the occasional flash of command. But it wasn't enough. Not for him. So he worked on her. Slowly. Patiently. Every day. Julian's dinners always ended in wine—not indulgence, but strategy. He knew a softened Claire was yielding, and every time he quietly downgraded himself before her, he was in fact upgrading the guilt that kept her blind to his game. And now she asked him to call her boss. Or did she order him to call her boss? Either way, it guided him where he finally wanted to be— a man provided for, carried even in his own work by her strength.

He waited until the business day was nearly over before making the call. Richard was surprisingly easy. They agreed quickly—next Saturday, 9 a.m., his studio. Fifteen hundred for a day's work. A neat victory. When Claire came home that evening, Julian, in his exaggerated, almost theatrical way, reported that her order had been carried out, the call made, the meeting arranged. She laughed it off, but he pressed, saying he owed her, that he'd pay her back by being her diligent boy after dinner, since she'd handed him a wealthy client. She laughed again, teased, tried to brush it away. But Julian didn't waver. The more he transformed her into a wife who gave commands, the more it thrilled him. Let her believe she ran the show. That was the sweetest illusion of all.

***

Julian arrived at the studio an hour early. He calibrated the lights, adjusted the softboxes, set reflectors in place, and made sure every backdrop and piece of décor he might need was within reach. Richard had been clear about his expectations: a life-size portrait, printed at the highest possible quality. Julian prepared accordingly. He selected the lenses most suitable for both close detail and dramatic full-length framing, double-checked his cameras, and even browsed a few creative references online to spark composition ideas.

When Richard finally appeared, Angela walked in beside him. Tall. Radiant. Eyes of a shark that seemed to strip everything bare. Julian froze. She was breathtaking, but she was also dangerous. The kind of woman he was subconsciously drawn to and instinctively feared. Real dominants terrified him because they didn't deal in guilt, the very currency his world was built on. Claire had guilt, which made her mouldable. Women like Angela had none. That made them lethal.

Julian offered them coffee or tea, but Richard only laughed, producing a few chilled bottles of champagne and a bag full of snacks. It was Angela's birthday, after all. They toasted, shared a laugh, and then Julian gently steered them toward the session. Angela was remarkable in front of the lens. She held her posture like a trained model, shifting her expression with a precision that stunned Julian—sultry one moment, aloof the next, playful, then distant. She understood her body, her face, the camera. Julian worked steadily, circling her, crouching low, shifting his angles and light. He was sweating within minutes. Richard, meanwhile, sipped champagne and occasionally leaned in with suggestions, directing both his wife and Julian as if the studio were his own. The more champagne he drank, the more theatrical he became—"Try it from the floor," "Make her look dangerous," "Get closer, closer, don't be shy."

After a couple of hours, they paused for a break, glasses refilled. And that was when Richard casually dropped it.

"Tell you something, Julian. Your wife is the bank's sharpest asset." He winked, taking a long sip. "Did you know she's one of five candidates for VP of Operations? That's a $1.1 million salary. Add bonuses, and she'll be netting close to two a year." Julian's chest tightened. His eyes widened, already calculating. Claire was earning six hundred thousand; this would easily double it. Richard watched him take it in, amused, as though observing someone face down an open jar of black caviar with an oversized spoon. The boy's hunger was obvious. Richard smiled to himself. Good. He was warming.

Then he clapped his hands, snapping Julian out of the fog. "All right, let's roll. I love it. Now, I want her on the floor, stretched as if on a bed. And you get down low, almost flat. I want the body at its sexiest, every line sharp. You can do that, right?"

Julian nodded, his camera steady but his mind consumed with one thought: Claire's new role. Richard's voice became the air he breathed. Every angle, every frame, every click of the shutter, all of it bled into the sound of Richard's command.

Working the camera, Julian barely noticed the sidelong glances, the whispered laughter, the winks exchanged between Richard and Angela. Their rhythm, their private sync, escaped him until it was too late.

"That's a great shot," Richard declared, clapping Julian hard on the shoulder after another hour of grueling artistry. "Remarkable work."

Julian smiled faintly, exhausted. "But…hey!" Richard's tone shifted. He pressed a little closer, steering Julian toward Angela, who lounged in the black leather chair. Her red dress clung to her like a new skin, hem riding high enough to draw every eye. Her legs were crossed with casual perfection.

"Look at this birthday girl," Richard said, his gaze fixed on Julian. "Isn't she gorgeous?"

"Oh, yes," Julian answered automatically. "The shots will come out great."

"Forget the shots." Richard winked, voice turning low, conspiratorial. "You've got a better shot than all of them right here." He chuckled at his own wordplay, then leaned in, eyes gleaming. "Go kneel in front of her. Service her. She's worked hard today. She deserves to ease the tension. Give her a birthday present." His hand pressed firmer into Julian's shoulder, pushing him forward.

Julian froze. "What?"

"You heard me." Richard's eyes narrowed, shifting into something predatory, cold. "Lick her. Otherwise…" He let the silence do the damage and then finished the sentence. "Otherwise… well, you know how these things work. One wrong step and it all vanishes."

Julian slowly turned to Angela. His body shivered, whether from the audacity of Richard's words or the thrill of feeling true domination for the first time. Brutal. Razor-sharp. Inescapable. He looked at her. The goddess. She was smiling an animal smile, raw and merciless. Slowly, consciously, she drew her dress up, revealing nothing beneath.

"Come, sweet boy," she purred. "Try this."

And then it happened. The arousal surged through him, sudden and violent. He couldn't fight it. The betrayal spread across his trousers, a dark, damp patch blooming over thin fabric. Angela saw it. She laughed, rich and triumphant, then beckoned again. Behind him, Richard's voice came sharp as a whip. "On your knees."

He hesitated a second or two and then dropped to the floor in front of her. He had no choice, he told himself. It was for Claire, his mind whispered. Then a sharp tug pulled him into place, and a silence followed. His world shrank to tongue, scent, heat, and Richard's breath, steady and close behind his ear. Then, Angela's convulsions, the rhythm of release. When it ended, Richard clapped his shoulder. 'That's my boy.'

Angela leaned forward, touched his lips with her wet fingers, then wiped her hand across his face as she rose. "We'll wait for the final prints," she said coolly. Richard added with a smile that never made it to his eyes, "You worked hard today. Keep your mouth shut, and Claire will get the job." His gaze lingered on Julian, still kneeling. "I know you will." With that, they left. The studio door closed behind them. Julian touched his face. Her taste was still smeared across his skin. Slowly, almost reverently, he licked the tips of his fingers. Downgraded, humiliated, scared… and yet, utterly, ruinously satisfied.

***

Richard kept his word. A few days later, Claire got the promotion. They celebrated with a short weekend trip to Vegas. Any other time, Julian would have used the escape to push Claire further into her role as a dominant wife, but this time, he couldn't bring himself to do it. Angela haunted him. A real goddess, wild and untamed, the kind who took without hesitation, without guilt, without shame.

Even after an exquisite dinner and expensive wine, he failed to move her toward his service. He didn't know if Claire expected it or not; she showed nothing and said nothing, but inside, he felt something broken. His body remembered Angela. His ears still echoed with Richard's filthy whispers as he performed. He carried that memory like a secret relic, dark and precious.

And then came the dinner that shattered him. He couldn't have possibly avoided it. He walked into their house with trembling hands, dread thick in his stomach. The giant portrait of Angela stared down at him like a witness. It stirred his mouth with the memory of her taste, and his trousers with something worse.

He watched them, Angela and Richard, play their private game in front of unsuspecting Claire. Angela's long gazes, her sly winks. Richard's mocking words echoed through his skull. "That's my boy." And finally, Angela's reckless performance. Julian fled to the washroom. But when he opened the door to return, she was there. Waiting. Richard and Claire were busy in conversation at the dining table. Angela said nothing. She only smiled, pointed down at her feet, and whispered: "Kiss." His chest tightened. He glanced around, panicked. Then dropped to his knees. His lips touched her shoe. She seized his hair, yanked his head up, pressed his face between her thighs. "Smell." He inhaled, dizzy. She released him as if discarding a toy, turned, and glided back toward the table. He stood frozen, eyes locked on the sway of her body.

When he returned, Claire seemed to notice nothing. But Richard knew. His wink told him everything. Julian managed a slow, defeated smile. He loved the game now consuming him, but feared the price it would demand.

And the price came a couple of hours later, in the car, when Claire asked him that question and touched him. He tried to play dumb. But his body betrayed him, and his erection gave him away.

For days, he turned it over in his mind, unable to understand why she did it. He was certain she knew nothing about the studio, nothing about Angela and Richard's games. Or... did she? Sometimes he wondered if she had known all along, if she had even sold him to her boss, rented him out, bartered him away like property. The thought both sickened and thrilled him. But clarity would come, cold and merciless. It was only his twisted imagination. Most likely, Claire knew nothing. Yet she must have felt something, some tremor of truth pulsing beneath the surface of their marriage. Whatever it was, the result was the same. She was gone. And Julian was left alone in their house, trying to puzzle out how to win her back.

Now Angela called. Out of nowhere. And once again, his world hung by a thread at the lip of an abyss he knew he was powerless to resist. Angela was beyond his will. A swarm of thoughts raced through his head. What did she mean? Something that might be interesting for both of us... The words looped in his mind, slippery and suggestive. Did she want him to do it again? For a split second, a wild thought flashed—he could, if she paid him. A lot. As if it were a service. He almost laughed at himself. Why would she pay when she could simply make him do it? She had leverage, and she knew it.

No, it didn't sound like play or sex. Her tone had been cooler, businesslike. Maybe it had something to do with photography, some clients she wanted to send his way. But then again, she could have just referred them. Angela was rich and busy. She wouldn't bother showing up here. Julian sometimes wondered what it would be like to be truly rich. But the thought always collapsed into the same conclusion: stupid. He never would be.

So, Monday, then. He would see her on Monday. Something inside him whispered he shouldn't press his luck with Claire, shouldn't send another text, shouldn't even stir the waters. With Angela's shadow looming, the smartest move was to stay low and invisible.

Chapter 14

The car was waiting when Claire stepped out of her building. Antonio stood beside it, leaning against the door as if he'd been rehearsing patience. His shirt was crisp, pale blue against his skin, no tie, sleeves folded just enough to suggest ease. When he caught sight of her, he straightened and smiled in a way that almost startled her—it was the same charming smile she remembered from the tennis courts. Or was it dangerous?

"Claire," he said, opening the passenger door as though she might refuse. She gave a nod, half a smile, and slid inside. The interior carried the faint smell of leather and something warmer, maybe his cologne, maybe the residue of him from last night. He joined her, started the engine, and for a few moments, silence filled the car. Claire's hands rested on her lap, steady in appearance but not in feeling. She couldn't quite find her role here. Not a girlfriend. Not a lover. Not even a colleague. Something else, undefined. It was the third time in her life that she had seen this man. And she already managed to have sex with him. That was crazy, Claire thought.

Antonio spoke first, his voice calm, "You look beautiful tonight."

She turned her head and offered the faintest smile. Compliments were easy currency. She had learned to accept them politely, never depositing them too deeply. "Thank you."

The city slipped past the windows. Antonio drove smoothly, one hand resting on the wheel, the other relaxed near the gearshift. His movements were efficient, yet there was nothing theatrical in them. She studied him for clues. Was this the same man who had pressed her against that wall in Jamaica? The same man who'd busted her lip? Or was this someone else entirely?

He seemed to sense her hesitation. "I'd like you to know who I am," he said. "The truth, not the version people in business invent."

Her gaze stayed fixed on the blur of streetlights. "And what version is that?"

"That I got lucky," he replied. "Or that I'm ruthless. Or that money builds itself if you're clever enough. None of it is true."

Claire glanced at him. His expression carried no bravado, only a quiet seriousness. She said nothing, letting him continue.

"I was married once. Six years ago, she left. No children. We had simply drifted. Nothing dramatic, no betrayal, just distance. Or maybe my work." He paused. "After that, I worked harder than I ever had. I built a company that specialized in one thing: software applications for banks. Nothing else. That was the key. While everyone else chased every industry, I stayed with one. Europe first. Then the expansion. We grew. Hundreds of millions in turnover." His eyes flicked toward her, then back to the road. "I sold it when an American firm came knocking. The money was outrageous. I invested much of it here, into Richard's bank. Into the future, I knew I could build for it. For us." He paused, smiled, "Since we are in the same boat now." Claire caught the last word. Us. She wondered if it was calculated.

"And now you still have your software products, right?" she asked, her voice even.

"Yes. Specialized banking apps. Online services. I believe they'll elevate this bank into something stronger." His tone was calm, matter-of-fact, not boastful. She could hear the truth in it, yet a whisper of doubt lingered. He wanted her to believe. She wasn't sure if she did. The traffic slowed near a light. He glanced at her again, this time longer, his eyes searching. "Tell me something, Claire. That night in Jamaica. Who was the girl?"

Her pulse stumbled. She shifted in her seat, reached for the window controls, and lowered the glass an inch as if the night air might steady her.

"A friend I met there," she said finally. But as she said it, the name Amanda burned in her mind, sharp and unyielding. For a flicker of a moment, she almost wanted to say it aloud, let the name hang between them, claim it, protect it. Instead, she swallowed it down, forced her tone flat.

He studied her profile, not pressing, though she felt the weight of his attention. He turned back to the road. "Whoever she was," Antonio said quietly, "she looked at you as though you were the only thing that mattered."

Claire forced a small laugh, casual, dismissive. "Jamaica was a blur."

But the name Amanda flashed across her mind, sharp as a cut, and she wondered how much Antonio had actually seen. They drove on, the silence no longer empty but charged. Claire folded her hands tighter in her lap, uncertain of herself, uncertain of him. Antonio spoke again, his voice softer now.

"I want you to know something, Claire, I'm here not because I... we... had sex, wild... raw really... No. I like you and I want to be with you. Nothing else."

She didn't have the words, didn't know what to say. The restaurant lights appeared ahead, glowing warm against the darkening sky. She felt her throat dry and lifted her chin. Tonight would demand clarity, and she wasn't sure she had any.

***

The maître d' guided them to a corner table, candlelight dancing against white linen. The restaurant had that polished hum of wealth with low conversations, discreet service, and the faintest notes of piano from the bar. Claire let Antonio lead. She didn't mind; sometimes, surrendering the choreography meant she could focus on reading the dancer.

With Julian, it had never been like this. He would wait, hesitate, glance at her for permission before sitting, before ordering, before even lifting the wine list. Without realizing it, she had been forced to direct every step, to carry the illusion of control he quietly scripted for her. It had become her second nature, eventually. She chose the wine, the courses, the rhythm of the evening, because if she didn't, the dinner collapsed into silence. Now, watching Antonio guide with ease, she noticed what she wasn't doing. She wasn't filling the gaps, wasn't propping up the structure of the night. He didn't need her to. The absence of that responsibility left a strange lightness in her, almost relief.

When the sommelier arrived, Antonio skimmed the wine list without hesitation and ordered a Bordeaux she recognized, not ostentatious, but seriously expensive. She wondered if it was a coincidence or a performance. For a while, the conversation was safe, about dishes, flavors, the city. Antonio had a talent for speaking without filling the air too heavily, letting silence breathe enough to feel considered, not empty. Claire studied the lines of his face when the light caught him, searching for cracks.

Halfway through the first course, Antonio leaned back, his glass in hand. "I told you about the company. But what I didn't say is how lonely it was. Building something like that... people admire you for the success, not for the years when you sleep in airports, when dinners are vending machines, when the only thing waiting at home is silence."

His tone was soft, almost confessional. Claire felt a stir in her heart, unwanted sympathy. She forced herself to stay neutral.

"You sold it at the right time," she said. "That takes foresight."

"Or luck," he countered. "But yes, timing mattered. The Americans wanted a foothold in Europe. I gave them that. And I got freedom." His gaze lingered. "Freedom to decide where I belong."

Her fork paused midway. He let the words sit there, unfinished but heavy.

The waiter cleared plates. Their eyes met across the candle. Antonio's look carried warmth, but beneath it, she caught something else. An intensity too quick to hide. A hunger, not for food. Claire shifted the conversation. "You said you were married once. Do you regret it ending?"

He shook his head slowly. "No. Regret isn't the word. We were young, ambitious in different ways. She wanted stability, children, and a husband who came home at six. I wanted to gamble everything on ideas, build something no one had tried before." His fingers tapped lightly on the stem of his glass. "But it taught me something. You can have everything, money, growth, recognition, and still be starving if you don't find the right person."

She looked at him carefully. His sincerity felt unguarded, almost raw. Yet part of her wondered if he had practiced this very line in another room, with another woman.

"And now?" she asked, tone deliberately light.

"Now I've built what I wanted. I don't need more. Except… someone to share it with." He looked at her. "Claire, I'm not playing games with you. I mean that."

The candle flame wavered between them. She sipped her wine, letting the richness linger on her tongue. Inside, her mind argued with itself. Part of her was tempted, drawn to the clarity in his voice. The other part whispered caution because men always sounded clear when they wanted to be believed. She smiled faintly. "You sound very sure."

"I am."

For a moment, silence wrapped the table. Claire felt the intensity of his gaze, not aggressive, not demanding. As if he were waiting for her to close the gap he had left open. She lowered her eyes to her plate instead. The second course arrived. Relief disguised as silver trays.

Claire rested her fingers on the stem of her glass, tracing a circle as though it might buy her courage. She didn't owe him anything, but Antonio's steady attention pressed gently at the edges of her silence. Finally, she spoke.

"I'm not officially divorced," she said, looking at the glass. "We separated. Months ago." She paused, choosing her words with care. "I used to think my husband was… different. Soft. Devoted. But now I'm not sure. Sometimes I wonder if he was playing a game I never saw. Making me believe I had to carry everything, money, choices, direction, while he stayed behind me, faithful, grateful, waiting for instructions."

Antonio didn't interrupt. His expression stayed calm, unreadable, except for the faint crease near his eyes, as if the gravity of her words mattered more than the polish of her delivery.

"I don't know if that's true," Claire added quickly, almost retracting the thought. "Maybe it's only in my head. But lately I caught myself wondering… if I've been living a story someone else wrote for me."

She let out a breath and gave him a rueful smile. "So I'm... experimenting, I guess. Trying to figure out who I am without him. What I want. Who I want. If I want at all."

Antonio tilted his head, then reached for his glass. His voice softened, touched with humor, just enough to loosen the tension. "Well," he said, "if experiments require volunteers, may I submit my candidacy? Full résumé available on request."

Claire laughed despite herself, the sound surprising her as it slipped out. "You're ridiculous."

"Persistent," he corrected, smiling, but he left it there. No insistence, no plea, only the faint echo of his joke hanging between them like a shared secret.

The evening ended quietly. Outside, he walked her to the car and opened the door for her. They drove almost in silence. He asked if he could call her. She said yes and gave him her number. Back at the apartment building, he didn't reach for her hand, didn't ask for another drink, didn't hint at anything more. Just a simple, warm, "Goodnight, Claire. Thank you for tonight."

She stepped into the elevator, the doors sliding shut with a soft seal. The mirrored wall caught her face, tilted in the light, tired, vivid, undecided. Antonio had asked for nothing, taken nothing. He'd left her with space, but in that space was a shadow she couldn't figure out yet. As the elevator rose, she heard the question again, the one Olivia had planted like a thorn: Who am I? And who do I want to be?

Chapter 15

Amanda sat on the couch opposite Claire, cradling a cup of tea. Her eyes brimmed with worry, glassy with the threat of tears. Her voice came soft, almost broken. "I feel awful about this. Truly."

Claire's reflective Sunday morning had begun with a bombshell: a call from Amanda, in the early hours. "Can we meet? It's urgent." Claire had frozen, the phone pressed to her ear. She had still been untangling her thoughts of last night with Antonio, and now Amanda was not only calling, but in town.

Claire looked at her and saw the trembling vulnerability, the guilt, and felt a wave of pity mingled with a dangerous desire to pull Amanda close, to soothe her, to protect her. What shook Claire most was not the confession itself but the gesture: Amanda hadn't hidden behind a text, hadn't made a call. She had flown to Chicago to say it in person.

The truth spilled out. Amanda's old life had resurfaced. Summoned her. She had resisted first, then faltered. She couldn't say no. Some force pulled her back, deeper than reason, older than choice. She needed to tell Claire face-to-face. She needed to say goodbye.

Claire set her cup down carefully, fingers lingering on the porcelain as if the warmth might anchor her. She drew in a breath, steadying herself, and when she spoke, her voice was even, almost too calm for the storm inside.

"Amanda... I've been doing a lot of digging lately into myself. And the truth is... I don't think I am what you need me to be... what you deserve me to be. I liked what we had... more than liked it. I let myself play with that power, I enjoyed it, I craved it in flashes... but when I strip it down, when I look at who I really am, I don't live in that place. Not the way you do. Not the way you need someone to."

Amanda's lips parted, but Claire lifted her hand, silencing her gently.

"You see, for me it was a play, an intoxicating play, but still... a play. I could wear the role, yes, and maybe even wear it convincingly. But a role is not a life. And for you, submission isn't costume. It's core. It's the thing your body will always circle back to, no matter how far you run. And I won't pretend I can hold that for you day after day. I won't trap you in a half-truth because I'm afraid to let you go."

Her voice thickened with emotion, but she forced it steady, pressing each word as though shaping it carefully for Amanda's sake.

"I care about you too much to make you live inside my limits. So if the man you once served has called you, if that's where your gravity pulls, then go. Don't carry me like guilt. Carry me as something you tasted, something real, but not the place you're meant to kneel."

Claire's throat ached as she stopped. The words had landed maybe sharp and intentional, but honest. She moved closer, sat beside her, and wrapped her arms around Amanda. Amanda gave her a tired, luminous smile. "You know," she whispered, "there was a moment when I thought I might be falling in love with you." Claire held her tighter. "Not just a moment. You did. And so did I. I'll always carry that with me."

They sat in silence, the kind that swells until it breaks. Then the tears came, and laughter through tears, and finally an embrace that pulled them back together. When they touched, it was without roles, without power, without leash or command. Tender, human, overwhelming—two women stripped of games, stripped even of shame.

By afternoon, Amanda had vanished from her world. Claire walked along the lake, the path crunching under her shoes, the air sharp with the smells of spring. Her body still carried Amanda's warmth. She had left as if answering a summons stronger than anything Claire could offer.

Claire thought back to those few hours. No leash, no commands. She had held Amanda as a woman, not as property. Equal. Human. Close. Tender in a way that rattled her more than domination ever had. Beneath it stirred fear—fear of something shifting inside her. And anticipation, too.

She shoved her hands into her coat pockets. Amanda had been pulled back into the orbit of a past that still claimed her. Yet Claire felt she wasn't lost forever. Whoever had taken her would one day loosen their hold, and Amanda would return. Claire carried that as fact. Still, a quiet, traitorous voice whispered that maybe Amanda would never come back. Maybe some leashes, once fastened, never truly loosen. She tilted her face toward the sky. The lake stretched wide and indifferent around her. Amanda's absence had left a hollow space, and Claire could only wonder what might one day fill it.

***

"Right," Olivia said, folding one leg over the other, her gaze steady on Claire. "So, Antonio is back in your life. That's quite a development."

Claire nodded. She had just told her everything about the coincidence at Richard's house, the dinner, and the date the next evening. And, of course, about Amanda, who had now drifted back into the orbit of her old life.

"I can't recall a weekend more intense for you," Olivia said, her tone neutral. "Let's try to make sense of it. First, how do you feel about Amanda?"

Claire bit her lip, shifted in the chair, as if bracing for impact. "I... made love to her. Not play, not domination. Just... love. And it's been bothering me."

"I see." Olivia leaned forward slightly. "What's the part that unsettles you most?"

Claire hesitated. "Before, it was power plays, performance. Not really sex, not... intimacy. This time it was different. Tender. And now I keep asking myself—does this mean I'm bisexual?" Her eyes lifted, questioning.

Olivia's expression softened. "What would be wrong if you were?"

Claire shrugged. "I don't know. Nothing, maybe."

"The worst thing you can do," Olivia said calmly, "is judge yourself. You acted on what you felt. That doesn't require a label right now. You've been exploring, and you're entitled to explore."

She paused, letting that land before continuing. "Now, Antonio. What did the date bring up for you?"

Claire exhaled sharply. "I think he's trying. My gut says he's a good man. What happened in Jamaica... I provoked it. He only played along. And I think I know why."

"Why?" Olivia asked immediately.

"Well..." Claire shifted again. "He mentioned Amanda. He doesn't know her name, but he asked who she was. I downplayed it, saying it was just a friend. But he admitted he'd noticed how she looked at me. So, at the restaurant, he must have picked up on that energy between us. Maybe he thought I was some kind of... sex-quest diva. That I was looking for the edge, so he played into it."

Olivia let the silence draw out, then asked quietly, "And were you?" Claire's throat tightened. She nodded slowly. "Yes. I was. I guess."

Both women felt it had been a good session. Claire was beginning to pull threads together, to name things that only weeks ago would have stayed buried. Clarity was close now, close enough that Olivia could sense it, even if Claire herself couldn't yet. Olivia shifted the focus. "And Julian? What's happening there?"

Claire shrugged. "Honestly, nothing. I didn't even reply to his text. And that tells me more than anything else."

"You're quite right," Olivia said with a small nod. "That silence speaks volumes about your priorities. Do you feel like you've let him go?"

"Maybe." Claire paused, thinking. "The thing is that Chloe's coming Friday, just for a few days. And it's inevitable I'll see him. Probably a family dinner, something like that. Chloe chose to stay at the house, so she'll be with him. I'll see her too… and I need to talk to her about all of this."

"Yes," Olivia said softly. "Clarity will matter for Chloe. And, Claire, tell me, are you going to sort out what you found in the bank statements? The lies you suspect?"

"Yes," Claire replied firmly. "I want closure on that. I want to know what actually happened in my marriage, in my life."

Olivia studied her for a moment, then spoke with unwavering calm. "Just be careful not to turn it into a circus. Or a fight. Keep it a conversation. An adult one. That's where the truth hides." Claire smiled at that word. Nearly fifty, and still reminded to act like an adult. The irony wasn't lost on her.

Chapter 16

Angela took the long, looping trail she walked every Saturday morning. Spring had warmed the trees. The air tasted of damp earth and green. She barely noticed. Her mind was busy. Last night's dinner with Claire and Antonio had not changed her plan so much as accelerated it. She was Richard Pollak's third wife. She had never intended to keep the title forever. She had not planned to exit this early either, but conditions were ideal. Richard was open. Too open. She had led him far into her own games, and he had followed gladly, the way men do when they think they are still leading. That brilliant little idea had been hers. The one she whispered into Richard's ear in the studio the instant the photographer disappeared into the back room. Make him kneel. Make him serve. It was Angela who suggested it, and Richard, drunk on champagne and her games, had obeyed. Now that moment was leverage, pure and simple. Before Antonio, it was worth something. After Antonio, its price climbed dramatically.

If Claire learned what Richard had made her husband do, the bank would choke on the scandal. With Antonio clearly on Claire's side, the Board would not protect Richard. Chair gone. Retirement plan bleeding. Money evaporating. Angela rolled the scenario on her tongue like a coin.

It needed polish. Pros and cons tested, timing chosen, an approach that presented itself as an offer yet left no space for refusal. Done right, it would buy her a clean exit and a far better settlement than any lawyer could pry loose. Richard was very wealthy. He also valued privacy and quiet.

Her mind wandered to a shoreline she had not picked yet. A Caribbean slip of sand. A house above the Pacific. Those were decisions for later. First, she needed Julian. On the trail, she stopped, took out her phone, and searched. His website surfaced in seconds. A studio number. She tapped it, listened to the ring, and smiled.

***

At breakfast on Monday, she was all smiles. She kissed Richard goodbye when he left for the bank and told him she was going shopping. "Buy something sexy," he called over his shoulder, and was gone. Fifteen minutes later, she slipped out too. Traffic was brutal, but she still reached the studio before ten. Julian was waiting.

The way his breath caught when she walked in was almost comical. He rose from his desk as if reporting to a senior officer.

"Hello," she said. He stammered something inaudible.

She sank into the armchair. "Put the Closed sign on the door. And lower the blinds."

He all but ran to obey. When he returned, she tilted her head, smiling in disbelief. "Why are you sitting? Shouldn't you be bringing me coffee?"

He bolted again, the sound of the machine hissing in the back room. Cups clinked. Moments later, he placed one in front of her.

"I'm sorry," he said, swallowing hard. "I… I'm still overwhelmed to see you."

"That's all right." Her smile stayed fixed, a little cruel.

He sipped nervously, then asked, "What can I do for you, Angela?"

She leaned back, voice carrying that ironic edge that made him shrink. "Let me be perfectly clear, Julian. I know what you're capable of. Last time you did a good job. And that's about all you can do for me." His stomach dropped. His tongue tensed. Somewhere in his trousers, something stirred.

"But..." She let the pause hang, enjoying it. "The real question is what I can do for you."

Her eyes locked on his. He nearly fainted. What can she do for me? His throat was sand. He wanted to speak, to ask, but nothing came. He just sipped and kept quiet.

"Look at you, Julian. Devoted. Quiet. A kind, reasonable man. No wonder they all use you. I heard Claire left. Distasteful, really. You worked yourself raw to make that woman shine, and this is the thanks you get? And Richard, your wife's boss, no less. He made you do it. I understand dominance. I loved watching you kneel. But I believe in balance. You give to me, I give to you. Wouldn't you agree?"

She tested him with her gaze. "Yes," he whispered.

"Good, Julian." Her smile sharpened. "Then I can offer you a partnership. Not equal, of course. I would still expect your service. But honest. Real. Isn't that who you are? A man built for service? You crave it, don't you? Serving the right woman. One who can truly take care of you."

Julian blinked, dazed. He couldn't follow where this was going. His voice cracked. "Can you... explain?"

"In a moment," she said lightly. "Get me another coffee first." He shot to his feet and hurried back to the machine.

Angela took the second cup and said evenly, "I can make you free, Julian. Give you a life that actually feels like yours. A life where you don't have to depend on unreliable people like Claire, people who only take and give nothing back." Her eyes lingered on him, probing.

"What did you get for all your loyalty? A separation. Because she grew tired of your dedication, tired of your service." She let a slow, sultry smile curl across her lips. "I bet you gave her everything. Worked hard. Pleased her. And in the end? She threw you away."

Julian sat frozen, pulse hammering. Angela leaned forward now, voice dropping to businesslike clarity. "Here's my offer. I'm divorcing Richard one way or another. And I thought of you, Julian. My settlement can be... considerably larger if we align our weapons."

He blinked, listening harder now.

"This is how I see it," she continued. "The studio… that photoshoot can be painted any way I like, Julian. A willing game, or an assault. A private thrill, or a scandal that burns down his career. Which version do you think Richard fears most? And if you stand with me, he will have no cards to play. He'll settle." Her gaze stayed locked on him. "You follow?"

Holy shit. Julian's head spun. Out loud, his voice cracked. "And… what's in it for me?"

Angela smiled her best boardroom smile. "Simple. I'll go after twelve million in cash. Two will be yours."

Julian blinked. Two million? Is she serious? The thought hit him like a drug. Two million could buy the life he'd ever truly wanted: modest, quiet, but entirely free. A clean little place. Days without obligations. Mornings with no plans. Just… nothing. Nothing at all. Two million dollars. Mine. Fuck.

"Can I… can I think about it?" he asked, cautious as a child testing a locked door.

"Fair enough," she said smoothly. "Sit on it. A couple of days enough?"

He nodded.

"Good. Text me by Wednesday afternoon. If you're in, we'll hammer out the details. If you're not..." Her eyes drifted across the studio, purposeful, dismissive. "...then you can spend the rest of your days hoping."

His mouth opened, then closed. He followed her gaze over the room, the cheap backdrops, the tired equipment. A cage dressed up as a workspace. The thought of rotting here, hoping for nothing, made his stomach twist. He was in. He already knew it. He just needed time to say it to himself. As she'd put it: sit on it.

"I'll be going, then," she said, but didn't move.

He looked at her. She looked back, her eyes demanding. It took him a few seconds to understand. The silence pressed. His pride screamed, but his knees bent anyway. He lowered himself, lips brushing the shine of her shoe. Rising a little higher, he pressed his lips against the silk of her stocking just below the knee. Her hand stopped him.

"You'll go higher when you're ready," she murmured. Then she rose, glanced down at him kneeling, smiled with triumph, and walked out the door.

***

Claire's Friday began with a text from Julian. A surprising one.

Can you pls pick up Chloe at the airport? I have an urgent photoshoot gig in LA and won't be back for at least a week. I'll call her as soon as she's home. Thanks.

A gig? In LA? That sounded about as likely as Julian flying off to Mars. Claire typed back *Sure,* but stared at the screen in disbelief. A gig instead of spending a few days with his daughter? She thought about asking if everything was all right, but let it drop. She'd hear soon enough. Maybe from Chloe.

At the arrivals hall, her heart swelled at the sight of her daughter—tall, radiant, hair spilling over her shoulders as she came smiling through the crowd. They hugged, kissed, and held on a moment longer than usual.

"Hey, Mom," Chloe said brightly. "How have you been?"

Claire smiled. "Busy."

"Dad?" Chloe asked.

"Didn't you get his message?"

"No… what message?"

"He's off to California. Urgent photo gig. Big bucks, I suppose."

Chloe stopped short, brows lifting. "Really? He didn't tell me a thing. I just spoke to him a couple of days ago."

"Yeah, well, he said he'd call you." Claire unlocked the car and gestured toward it. "Come on, let's get moving."

On the drive, Claire kept her tone light. "Honey, you don't mind staying with me, right?"

"No problem, Mom. Let's just swing by the house and grab some things."

"Of course," Claire said. "We'll stop there first, then head to my place."

They reached the house. Chloe wanted to collect a few things from her room, clothes mostly, before moving into Claire's condo. She had hoped to stay here. That had been the plan. But with Julian gone, there was no choice. Asking her mother to move back just so she could feel at home would have been absurd.

They sat together at the spotless kitchen counter, two glasses of water between them. Claire studied her daughter's face.

"I know you'd rather stay here," she said quietly.

"That's okay, Mom."

Claire breathed in. She owed Chloe an explanation, yet she hadn't rehearsed one. This was the moment, though. It couldn't wait.

"Honey," she began, her voice uneven, "I want you to know something. I'm… responsible for what happened. The separation. It was my decision. You already know that, but I need you to hear it from me."

Chloe nodded. "I know, Mom. And… you have the right to change your life if you need to. I get it. I'm not a child anymore." She managed a small smile. "I understand."

"Still," Claire pressed gently, "even grown women need clarity. And I wish I could give you a neat explanation, but I can't. I don't have a solid base to build one on. I acted on a feeling." She paused, sipped from her glass. "And it's been a strange one."

"What feeling?" Chloe asked. Her eyes stayed fixed on her mother's, searching.

Claire lifted her shoulders helplessly. "The feeling that I wasn't living my own life. That it was... directed. Streamlined into something I hadn't chosen. I never stopped to ask why things were the way they were. I was busy, and I kept going with the flow. And now I'm asking myself if my life was ever really mine."

"Why are you saying that, Mom? Didn't you do what you wanted?"

Claire was silent for a moment. "Yes... and no. That's the trouble, Chloe. When I ask myself if I wanted a career without balance, my answer leans toward no. When I ask if I wanted to carry the weight of every major decision, the money, the property, your education, again, my answer is no. Not like that. Not all alone."

Her voice thinned. "And I wouldn't have minded carrying it, Chloe, if I hadn't been lied to."

Chloe straightened, alarm flashing. "What do you mean? Did he... cheat on you?"

"No." Claire shook her head firmly. "No one cheated. Not that kind of lie. Something different." She drew a breath. "Years ago, before you were born, your dad told me he'd invested his savings in his photography equipment. That his uncle sold it to him, and that's why he couldn't help with the rent. In reality, the equipment was a gift. He never paid a cent. He just said that to explain why he wasn't contributing."

Chloe's lips parted. "Wow. How do you even know that?"

"I found bank statements by accident," Claire said. "Regular deposits from his mother, two thousand every month. No payouts for equipment. No withdrawals. Nothing. So I called his uncle's wife. She confirmed it. The equipment had been a gift."

Chloe's voice cracked. "But... why would he lie?"

"That's what I don't know." Claire leaned closer, searching for words. "Imagine a child and an adult. The child doesn't know enough, so it's easy for the adult to convince them that white is black. That's how I feel. As if I'd been guided into decisions that weren't really mine, led along like a child, making choices that served someone else's agenda." She hesitated. "Maybe I'm not explaining it right. But that's the truth of how it feels."

Chloe sat wide-eyed, stunned. Then she whispered, "Maybe I do understand, Mom."

She put her water glass down and slipped toward her room without another word. Claire watched her go, her throat tight, knowing the conversation had only just begun. Chloe came back carrying a small pink notebook with a broken spiral and stickers peeling off the cover. She flipped through quickly, then stopped.

"Here, Mom." She slid it across the counter. "Maybe this is what you meant."

Claire looked at it. Across the page, in big uneven letters, was the voice of a child:

Big mystery in my house. I want to be a detective when I grow up. I don't want to solve murders because I hate blood. But mysteries like today. Mom left for London for work. But she had a big problem. She lost her passport. She was running up and down the house all morning looking for it. Then Dad found it in Mom's car. But here is the mystery! Yesterday before bed I came downstairs to get a bottle of water. I saw Mom's purse on the floor by the stairs. And next to it was her passport. I even read the word on it PASSPORT. So how did it get in Mom's car? Impossible. I asked Dad when Mom left. He said I was wrong and that I saw something else. But how could he know? He didn't see it. I did.

Claire's hands trembled as she finished the page. Her eyes burned. Could an eight-year-old have invented this? Misread something? Mistake a passport after sounding out the word on the cover? Very unlikely. And there had only been three people in the house. If she hadn't lost the passport in her car, then...

She let out a long breath. And then... the puzzle pieces of her marriage neatly aligned in her mind. She understood the depth of it. The tragedy of it. She forced a tired smile, tried to lighten her voice. "You were quite the detective, honey."

But Chloe's eyes stayed fixed, unblinking. "Do you remember that?"

"I do," Claire said softly.

"The whole 'child–adult' thing you mentioned now... it brought back this memory. When I was little, I wrote it down and never showed anyone.

Maybe even then, I knew not to. Maybe I felt something was wrong, but I couldn't put it into words."

Claire said nothing. She had no answer. Chloe stood, her face pale. "Why would he do that, Mom? What was the game about?"

"I don't know," Claire admitted. Then, after a pause: "Guilt. Control. Gratitude. Maybe all three."

"That's sick, Mom."

Claire picked up her bag. Her voice was flat now. "We need to go, Chloe. I think I've had enough memories for one day."

Chapter 17

Julian was on the beach. Forget Los Angeles. He was in Florida. Angela, his new partner, his new boss in every sense, had arranged everything. It started after he sent her a text with just three words: *I am in.* They met, hammered out the details, and Angela made the first move: keep him invisible. No contact with Claire, no loose conversations with anyone. Julian knew Chloe was arriving in two days, so he had to disappear quickly. His solution was the same dingy motel as before. He stayed there for nearly a week until Angela called with the next step.

They met her lawyer. A sharp man, efficient, clinical. He walked them through the plan: Julian was to sit tight until Angela had Richard's agreement in writing. Once her divorce settlement was finalized and filed with the court, Julian would make his move. He would serve Claire with divorce papers and, at the same time, a settlement agreement. It was clean: he'd waive any rights to property or joint assets, give up the house, give up cash. No contest. No fight. Judges liked uncontested divorces, and they moved quickly through the system.

The key was sequencing. Richard would first pay Angela's settlement. From that, two million would be placed in an escrow account under the lawyer's control. When the judge signed Julian's uncontested divorce decree, the money would be released. A new bank account, his name only, and freedom, no questions, no loose ends.

It sounded airtight. Too airtight. Which was exactly why Julian liked it. He signed the representation agreement with the lawyer, then pocketed the twenty thousand in cash Angela had advanced him. It wasn't just money for him; it was proof. Proof that she trusted him. Proof that he was finally being treated like a man of worth. Two days later, he was on a flight to Miami with nothing more than a carry-on and an address scrawled on a slip of paper. Angela had arranged that too. The apartment was high above the water, with glass walls, white leather, the kind of place he would never have dared to imagine for himself. Stay here, she'd told him. It belongs to a friend. We'll have it as long as we need. His instructions were simple: keep out of sight, wait for the papers to move through the system. Meanwhile, she told him, he should think about what came next. Do you want to stay in the States? Mexico? Europe? Decide where you want to start fresh.

Julian was ecstatic. Each morning, he walked the beach, the Florida heat soaking into his skin, dreaming of futures he hadn't yet chosen. No rent to worry about. No studio, no clients, no Claire with her stupid blow job questions. Just the sound of waves, the illusion of freedom, and Angela somewhere in Chicago working to crack the safe.

He was almost relieved that his attempt to guilt Claire back hadn't worked. He hadn't pushed hard, true, but she hadn't reacted either. That stung. He'd grown used to winding her around his finger with a glance, a sigh, a carefully timed silence. Not this time. Still, it didn't matter. Not anymore. Now he was finally on the path to something bigger, his own real play. His chance at redemption. Proof to everyone else that he wasn't the pet they believed Claire had shaped him into.

He called Chloe and spun a clumsy lie about the LA gig—something about a colleague needing backup on a high-profile shoot, maybe tied to a film, hinting vaguely at Hollywood. Chloe didn't sound impressed. If anything, her voice was cool, reserved. Julian didn't mind. She was grown now, nearly out on her own. It was time he thought about himself. Besides, he knew the endgame: he'd leave Claire's assets uncontested. Chloe would be fine. More than fine. In his mind, abandoning the fight looked almost like generosity. He tugged the brim of his cap down over his eyes and kept walking along the sand, letting the Florida sun burn him bronze. A perfect tan for a brand-new life.

***

"Do you like wine, Claire?" Antonio asked, holding a Starbucks cup in his hand. The contrast made her laugh. "Well… yes. Why?"

"Because someday," he said, "I'd love to take you home. To Italy. My family has vineyards."

"Oh…" She tilted her head, then teased, "So you're not poor." She chuckled at her own joke.

Antonio laughed with her. "No. I've never been poor. But I always had a different drive. I wanted to build something myself. Not wine. I love wine, but working in it… not my cup of…" He lifted his paper cup with a smile. "Cappuccino."

She laughed again, shaking her head.

"And I am richer than my parents now."

"And much more modest, too," she added with a grin.

"I don't shy away from success," he said playfully.

They strolled along the lake, coffees warming their hands. Antonio's energy was open, steady, and hopeful. Claire's was quieter, layered. She wasn't pushing him away, but she wasn't pulling him close either. She was listening to herself. And what she heard was noise—Julian's shadow, Amanda's skin, the unanswered questions about her own marriage, her own desires. Did she want another relationship? Another marriage? Not really. Did she want freedom to explore? Possibly. Did she want Amanda again? That thought burned, not just in her mind but lower, deeper, in the body she didn't entirely trust. It scared her.

And Julian... Everything about him was unfinished, unresolved. She ached for closure, for clarity. He was away in LA, leaving her to circle the silence. Chloe had stayed for a few days, then gone back to Boston, back to her own life. Claire had told her she'd help if she wanted her own place there. Now it was only her work left, sessions with Olivia, and Antonio.

He didn't press. He walked beside her, waiting.

"Let me tell you something, Antonio." She stopped, looked at him. Her eyes were serious now. "That thing in Jamaica. It was my fault. I thought I wanted danger. And then when it happened, I realized it wasn't danger. It was damage. And I can't unsee that."

Antonio nodded. He didn't speak. He didn't want to prod where words could cut. He knew he had to be careful. This wasn't a woman to risk with careless honesty or hunger.

"I understand, Claire," he said finally. "More than you think. You need time. That's fine with me. I'll wait, if you let me. And if you ever decide to give me a chance, I'd be at your door that same moment." Her smile came, amused and a little disarmed. No one had ever said that to her before.

"If you don't mind me asking… how old are you, Antonio?" Claire's tone was light, but her eyes held him steady.

"Forty-two," he said.

"And I'm almost forty-nine." She let the numbers hang between them, then added, "In ten years, I'll be sixty, very likely a grandma with a grandchild or two. And you'll be just past fifty, full of life, looking at young, beautiful women. Have you ever thought about a future like that?"

He exhaled, slow and steady. "I don't know what ten years will bring, Claire. All I know is what I feel right now. When I saw you at that restaurant in Jamaica, something clicked. Something lit up in me, and I thought: that's my woman. That's the woman I want next to me. Maybe it sounds childish. Maybe romantic. But it was true then, and it's true now. I don't care how old you are."

She arched a brow, testing him. "Well… you don't now…" He held her gaze, unflinching. "I never will. Love doesn't measure age."

Something surged in her, sudden and dangerous. She wanted to kiss him. But she didn't. Many years ago, she had stumbled into the same desire when Julian showed her a photograph of herself, a true masterpiece. Back then, she hadn't stopped. She kissed. Now, by the same lake, she heard words shaped with the same artistry, words that felt like a masterpiece in sound. This time, she didn't rush. Finally, I've grown up, she thought, and a sad smile touched her lips.

Chapter 18

The chessboard gleamed, every piece perfectly aligned, like everything else in Richard's house after the cleaners had left. Angela sat in the lounge with a dry martini, her gaze fixed on the board. She didn't play. She plotted.

Richard wouldn't be home for another hour. The silence gave her time to prepare. All the puzzle pieces were arranged, neat and orderly, just as she liked them. When Julian's text arrived, she had smiled. She'd known he would cave before he even realized it himself. She recognized the type. She knew the flaws. Men were her specialty.

But this scheme demanded more than her own cleverness. Careful planning, precision, and backup. She had already called her brother in San Francisco, the only person she trusted without question. He had helped before, during Angela's previous marriage, the one before Richard, the one she walked away from with six million in her pocket. He'd be arriving early next week.

Now, all that remained was the final act: the performance with Richard. Timing mattered. She knew his patterns. In the morning, when his testosterone was low, he was lucid, pragmatic, all business. At night, with his body pushing him, he grew rash, arrogant, and easy to manipulate. To strike in the morning, she would first have to stage the evening. But it couldn't look like seduction. To stir even the faintest trace of guilt in him, it had to feel like his own indulgence, his own excess. She had a plan.

When Richard came home, he stopped in his tracks. Angela, in a fitted top and her tightest yoga pants ever, was on all fours with a towel, scrubbing beneath the cabinet. "What are you doing?" he asked, mesmerized by the curve of her body. Angela kept wiping beneath the cabinet, a queen disguising herself as a pawn.

Without turning, she said coolly, "I'm not happy with the cleaning lady. She misses things."

Richard didn't believe a word about the cleaning lady. Since when had Angela cared about a little dust under a cabinet? Nonsense. What he saw in front of him was an invitation, another one of her games, and he loved every single one of them. "Well, I'm happy," he muttered, moving closer. "If Lupita's little faults make you crawl around in those pants... Jesus..." His hand slapped against her butt. "She'll get a raise for it."

"Leave it, Richard," she said, her voice carrying just the faintest note of play. "Leave it?" he scoffed. "Are you fucking kidding me?" His hands grabbed her firmly. "Stay there."

"No, Richard. I said leave it." But he didn't listen. Her pants slid down to reveal nothing underneath. "Dear God! Look at you!" He whispered and traced his finger along the most delicate line he had ever known. "Richard, I told you, don't start now. I'm busy," she said. He only chuckled. He loved the setup, loved her for being so fucking inventive. His fingers fumbled at his buttons, and then he drove into her with a force that tore a gasp from her throat. Exactly as she had planned.

He heard the edge in her voice but took it as he always did, twisting refusal into consent, mistaking strategy for play. "Oh, you love it when I take you like this, don't you?" She moaned just enough, a mixture of protest and performance, and held her composure, though release clawed at her. She was ready to come, but she fought it. This wasn't the moment to reveal how much she enjoyed him. When it was over, she played the role to perfection: storming off, pretending to be upset, retreating to bed early, leaving him downstairs with the television and a bottle of whiskey he drowned himself in. He thought he'd taken her. In truth, she'd only given him a pawn. Tomorrow, she would take the king.

***

Angela came down late to breakfast, her best unhappy mask fixed in place. Richard was already at the table, serving pancakes, pouring Prosecco, his version of an olive branch. It was a Saturday morning that might have been beautiful, but she had other plans.

She sat without a word.

"Hey," Richard said lightly. "Stop being an angry bee."

"You don't get it, Richard. You never listen to me."

"I always do. You lead our games, and I love them."

"I think I want to end them," she said coolly.

"What? Why?" He froze mid-bite, pancake balanced on his fork.

"I want out, Richard."

"Out of what?" He still wasn't catching on.

"Out of the marriage."

He nearly choked. "This some kind of new game?"

"No. I'm serious."

The fork clattered onto the plate. He set down his cutlery, dabbed his mouth with the napkin, his face calm, but his blood was heating. He studied her. "So you're saying you want to end our marriage?"

"Yes."

"May I know why?"

"Richard… you're a great man. You're fun. But my life has become trapped around yours. And that's not how I picture myself. I want to do things for myself. Do you understand?"

He nodded once, hard. "What stops you from doing that now? Married or not?"

"Well, nothing and everything. I feel like my only purpose has been making your life full, rich, and entertaining. Like last night. You took what you wanted, had your own fun without asking if I wanted it."

He sat in silence for a long beat, wondering if yesterday's episode was worth ending the marriage over. It certainly wasn't, no matter which way you looked at it. The thought struck him: she was using her yoga pants trick to stir the muddy waters. Maybe to get something out of him, maybe something else. Either way, the thought promised nothing good. Aloud, he said, "So you just want to walk away?"

"Not exactly." Her voice sharpened. "I think we should talk about what's fair. Six years with you, Richard, and I gave you all I could. I expect you to appreciate that."

Finally, it clicked in his head. Forget love. It was business. A sour taste rose in him because if this was business, then she had seen their marriage as nothing more than a wife-for-hire contract. That stung. But he didn't let it show.

"Right," he said carefully. "What do you have in mind?"

She shifted in her chair. "I want a quiet, amicable divorce. No drama. We walk away clean. Twelve million in cash, and I waive everything else."

"What? Twelve million?" His voice rose, stunned. His face turned red.

"You're a wealthy man. You have more than that, I know it. Twelve is fair."

"Fair? Are you fucking insane?"

She met his glare, steady. "Do I look insane to you, Richard?"

He stopped. Drew in breath. Focused. "No. You don't."

"Exactly. And here's why. You have a brilliant career, Richard. A great life. Don't ruin it."

"What the hell does that mean?"

Her smile turned into pure poison. "No one has to know what happened in that studio on my birthday. Right? Especially Claire. Especially now."

The bomb landed with brutal force. Explosion, then silence. Richard's mind snapped to the picture instantly. He was no fool. He saw exactly what she was playing with. He rose and tossed his napkin aside. It took him all his strength to control himself. He managed his tone level, almost cold: "And what stops Claire's husband from telling her about it anyway?"

Angela's smile widened, dazzling and merciless. "I do." He froze. Then gave a short nod. "Of course. So, you got to him first. I see how this goes. You planned this whole deal."

He paced the room, heat running through his veins, but he still kept his cool. He knew better than to explode here. After a long silence, he said evenly, "I'll be gone a couple of days. Back Monday. Then we'll hammer out details. Deal?"

"Sure, darling. I love when you're all business." Her voice turned syrup-sweet. She winked at him. Richard slipped into his jacket, left without another word, got in his car, and called his lawyer.

***

Matthew Hammond had been Richard's lawyer and his closest confidant for decades. When Richard called and said it was urgent and that they needed to fly to Vegas, Matthew didn't ask why. He asked only one question: "What time?" Richard said he'd pick him up in an hour.

Now they sat side by side in a shadowy row of slot machines, the casino floor half-empty, time suspended. They pressed buttons, watched the reels spin, and talked business. Well, Richard talked. Matthew listened, chiming in only with the occasional pointed question. Vegas always cleared Richard's head. He didn't know why; he just knew it worked. Both of his first two divorces had been settled here. And now, the third one was already writing itself into history. Richard laid it all out. About the games Angela had taught him to play. About the studio setup. About that drunken whisper in his ear: I love when you make people serve me. Now I want a special kind of service.

He remembered grinning like an idiot, drunk on the feeling of power she gave him, the illusion he could do anything, even make another man kneel for her. Back then, it felt thrilling. Now, it just felt dangerous.

Her timing was perfect. She had seen the moment Antonio and Claire became connected, and with that, she knew Richard's armor had cracked. The studio incident could ruin him. If she had Julian on her team, and Richard was certain she did, then she held a weapon sharp enough to cut through his career. The bank's board wouldn't hesitate. His reputation would collapse. He'd be forced to step down, stripped of influence overnight. He ran the math quickly, as always. The losses would run to at least fifteen, maybe twenty million, over the next three years. He wanted to retire, yes, but on his own terms, preserving the fruit of his work, not splitting it with a vulture who had spent six years fattening herself at his table.

Matthew absorbed it all quietly, his expression neutral. He had seen it all before. At last, he spoke, voice calm, grounded. "I'll have solutions ready by breakfast. Whatever happens, Richard, you won't be walking into this unarmed." Richard nodded, eyes fixed on the spinning reels. He knew one thing for sure: his life had changed.

***

The following morning, at breakfast, Matthew sipped his black coffee, leaned back, and said, "Here's how I see it, Richard. On one side, we've got twelve million dollars. On the other side, there is a serious reputational risk if she decides to go public. Without overcomplicating it, the cleanest move is to take the deal, but on very strict terms. The settlement agreement will be airtight. She'll get her money, yes, but in exchange, she waives any right to speak about your personal life. Not to the press, not to a friend, not even to a dog. Absolute confidentiality, backed by serious financial penalties if she breaches."

Richard narrowed his eyes. "And you think that's her endgame?"

Matthew nodded. "That's what we'll test. If she signs, the money flows, I'll funnel the papers through a judge I know well, and the divorce sails through uncontested. Once the decree is entered, you're clear. And she's gone. Simple as that."

Richard rubbed his chin. "I hope so. What about Julian?"

Matthew's expression darkened slightly. "He's trickier. If he decides to talk, it's technically his word against yours. Angela would be gagged by the agreement, but he wouldn't. Theoretically, he could file something in court. But let's be realistic. Litigation takes money and time, and from what you've told me, Julian has neither. That said," He lifted a finger. "We'll dig. If Angela has promised him a cut, that gives us leverage. We can either expose it or use it to corner him."

"Can we make him sign something, too?" Richard asked. Matthew thought a moment. "Possibly. A separate NDA. Tie it to a payout if Angela insists he's part of the picture. Something with heavy liquidated damages, say a few million, if he opens his mouth later. Not bulletproof, but enough to scare him quiet."

Richard nodded slowly. "All right. What's next?"

"I'll need two hours with my team," Matthew said. "By the time you've bled a little more at the tables, we'll have a draft ready. Then we move."

"Deal," Richard muttered.

After breakfast, they split. Matthew went upstairs to his suite to work on the draft, and Richard headed back to the casino floor. By the time Matthew found him, Richard was grinning like a fool, fifteen thousand in cash stacked in front of him from a lucky slot machine. Richard raised his glass, "See?" he laughed. "The universe always pays me back. I knew I made the right call." Matthew didn't smile. Just handed him the draft agreement. He knew better than to mistake luck for strategy.

Chapter 19

"In fact, I tried to reach him, Olivia," Claire said. "I wanted to set up a meeting, talk things through. No luck. The only reply I got was that he was busy and preferred to wait until he got back."

Olivia leaned in slightly, attentive. "And where is he supposed to be now?"

"He said LA. Some kind of photoshoot gig that was meant to take a week. But it's been three, maybe more."

Olivia nodded slowly. "That does sound like avoidance. What's your sense of why?"

Claire lifted her hands, then let them fall again. "He's been acting strange. I don't know... Maybe he suspects I saw those bank statements. Maybe something else." She hesitated. "And yesterday, something odd happened. Richard asked me about him. Out of nowhere."

Olivia's voice stayed calm, curious. "What exactly did he ask?"

"If I knew where Julian was. I told him no. Then I asked why. He brushed it off and said someone wanted a portrait like Angela's, the one they keep in the house." She shook her head. "But would Richard really be looking for Julian himself? Doesn't add up. At most, he'd give the name of the studio. It's online, anyone can find it."

"I see," Olivia said evenly. "So what do you make of that sequence of events? Julian has been gone longer than he said. Richard suddenly asks after him?"

Claire pressed her lips together. "Honestly? I have no idea."

Olivia tilted her head. "Could this tie back to that dinner? The night you asked the question. You sensed a dynamic between Julian and Richard. Now Richard is suddenly asking about him. What does your gut say?"

Claire sat up straighter. "I've thought about that too. It does feel like something's happening behind the curtain, something I can't see."

"Or something you don't want to see," Olivia suggested gently. Claire fell quiet. Olivia topped up their mugs with coffee, then shifted gears. "Let's talk about Antonio. How do you feel when you're with him?"

"Honestly? He's fun. Easy to be with." She paused, searching for the right words. "But I can't shake the feeling I'm edging myself into a corner. That at some point, I'll have to give him a yes or a no. He hasn't pressured me, but it's there. He wants clarity. He's hinted at more than attraction. He even said love doesn't measure age…"

"That's telling," Olivia said. "And you're already anticipating the moment you'll be asked to decide."

"Exactly." Claire let out a breath. "I don't feel ready for that." Olivia studied her with a trained, professional eye. "No, you are not."

Olivia took a sip of coffee, then set the mug down carefully. "Claire, I've left the most crucial part of our conversation until now. Let's talk about your time with Chloe, the passport story, and her reaction to it."

Claire drew in a long breath. "That was heavy, Olivia. Probably the hardest moment I've ever had with her. Looking at her face while she pieced things together about her own father, asking me those questions… it was brutal."

Olivia nodded. "I can imagine. You both recognized that the passport story wasn't innocent. Chloe opened a box she didn't even know she was holding, and what came out was ugly: the truth about her own family. Tell me, Claire... do you understand why he did that?"

"Yes," Claire said, lowering her eyes as if she felt shame instead of Julian. "I do. When I read Chloe's little note, it was like every puzzle piece I'd been ignoring finally clicked. Not only about the passport, but my entire life."

She stared at her hands for a couple of long seconds, then continued. "I can see now how he shaped me into something I never wanted to be. How he slipped in guilt, drop by drop, until I believed I was lucky to have my choices. He made me think I pursued my career freely, that climbing the ladder was mine." Claire's voice broke. She reached for the cup, as if it could steady both her hands and her scattered thoughts. Olivia helped her anchor it. "So he built the illusion of freedom, but it was really control."

"Absolutely! And you know, he praised me for my success constantly, relentlessly. But it wasn't about me. It was never about me. It was about him. In his eyes, I was simply the boss he needed to keep happy, so his own little world could keep running." Olivia listened, then gave a measured nod. "I think you've named it. You see it now for what it was. But seeing it is one thing, Claire.

Deciding what to do with it is the next step." Claire stayed silent, weighing the question she dreaded most: whether she was ready to take that next step.

***

Richard came back home late Monday morning. Angela didn't rise to meet him. She was sprawled in a patio chair, sunglasses on, thumbing through her phone. He stepped outside, dropped a stack of papers onto the coffee table, and said without preamble, "Here. Your ticket to a new life. Enjoy." Then he turned and walked back in.

Angela picked up the papers and flipped through them quickly. Her lawyer would scrutinize every clause, but even at a glance, she could tell Richard was caving without a real fight. The nondisclosure provisions, the bans on media, the restrictions on sharing anything about their private lives, none of it bothered her. She didn't care to dig up their past. She only wanted a clean exit with the money. From what she saw, she might actually get it. She lingered on one detail: she was barred from removing anything from the house except for a short, itemized list. The portrait Julian had done of her wasn't on it. Interesting.

She called her lawyer, set up a meeting, and slid the agreement into her bag. Then, testing Richard's temperature, she went inside. He was at the machine, pouring coffee.

"Since everything seems to be falling neatly into place between us," she said lightly, "why don't we celebrate?" He turned. For the first time in years, she couldn't read his eyes. "The divorce, you mean?"

She smiled, syrupy and cruel. "Divorce is one thing. Fun is another. She sauntered a step closer.

Richard froze with a cup in hand. His answer came flat, almost calm. "Will forty-eight hours be enough for you to move out?" She stopped, stared at him with a look that was equal parts seductive and venomous. Then she turned and walked upstairs without a word. He watched her go, her hips moving like a dare, and allowed himself the faintest smile. Chapter three was now officially closed.

***

They stepped out of the cineplex into the velvet-dark night, the air faint with the scent of popcorn and rain still drying on the pavement. Claire tucked her scarf tighter around her neck, her heels clicking against the concrete as Antonio fell into step beside her. They had just seen Challengers, the film that had critics calling it dangerous and erotic, a tangle of ambition and desire played out on a tennis court. It had left Claire both stirred and thoughtful, her body humming with its energy. Antonio broke the silence first. "The way they carried that tension… always there, never resolved until the very last moment… it reminded me of us."

Claire glanced at him, amused but cautious. "Yes. The restraint. And then the leap. But let's be honest, Antonio, those leaps don't always end well. At least mine didn't in Jamaica."

He smiled, but his eyes held a trace of seriousness. "Sometimes they end exactly the way they should. Maybe they teach us something."

They walked toward the restaurant he had chosen, a small Italian bistro tucked behind a row of boutiques. Candlelight flickered inside, and when they stepped in, the warmth of roasted garlic and fresh bread wrapped around them. A corner table was waiting, intimate and discreet. The conversation flowed easily at first. They discussed the film, the cinematography, and the audacity of the love triangle. Claire teased him about analyzing it like a playbook, and he laughed, enjoying her quick wit. But beneath the banter, Antonio was searching, probing for something more solid.

"When she held that racquet," he said, swirling the wine in his glass, "it wasn't about sport. It was about waiting for someone who could match her energy. That struck me, really."

Claire arched a brow. "Oddly specific." She gave a soft laugh, but then her eyes dropped to her plate. "Though yes, I felt it too."

He leaned in slightly. "How do you feel about us, Claire?" The candlelight sharpened the lines of his face, made his sincerity harder to dodge. Claire chose her words with care. "I feel... captivated. You're easy to be with, Antonio. But I also feel I'm still figuring out what I want. I don't want to rush into something that feels right only because it's easy."

He absorbed that, tried to mask the flicker of disappointment with a gentle nod. "I understand. Even if my heart wants to move faster." Claire smiled, soft, almost apologetic. "That's not your fault. I'm just not used to knowing exactly what I want. I think I've been expertly shaped into someone I never truly was."

Dinner lingered over two courses and a shared dessert, laughter weaving through their restraint. Yet every time Antonio tested the edges, reaching for her hand, speaking about the future. And Claire... Claire shifted, subtle but unmistakable.

When they finally stepped back out into the night, the city had gone to sleep. At her car, Antonio paused. For a moment, he thought she might let him hold her, kiss her, close the distance. Instead, she leaned in with the briefest touch of lips against his cheek.

"Goodnight and thank you," she said. He returned it softly. "Goodnight. I am already planning our next date." She smiled at his words. He stood there watching her slide into her car, a dull ache knocking on his heart. Of course, he would wait. He was already in love with her. There was no denying it. He wanted her as his girlfriend, his partner, someone to wake up next to. He could see their life so clearly, even the ordinary mornings. But tonight made him wonder if that would ever happen at all. Maybe she would never let him in. Maybe he was waiting for something that would never come. The thought hollowed him.

As she drove away, her hands tightened on the wheel. Antonio was everything she should want. Warm, attentive, steady. Part of her longed to pull into his arms, to let sex dissolve the uncertainty. But Jamaica still burned in her memory—the unfinished, the raw, the too-much-too-soon. It stopped her cold. She wasn't ready, not yet. She needed time, clarity, something more than desire. Tonight had been good, even beautiful. But she knew herself well enough to sense it. If she gave in too quickly, she'd ruin it. And she didn't want to ruin it. Somewhere deep inside, she knew her hesitation might cost her. Antonio wasn't the kind of man who would linger forever, no matter what he promised. And yet, even with that risk, she couldn't bring herself to leap.

***

Surprisingly, the motel didn't look quite as ugly this time. Julian dropped his bag on the bed and reached for his phone. Angela's message had pulled him back from the sun into business. It was time to act.

She confirmed the deal was signed, the papers already moving through the court. It wouldn't take long, she said. Now it was Julian's turn. First, find yourself a lawyer, she had told him. Not ours. One just for the divorce. Your case is simple: waive everything, walk away free. Then collect your reward and build a new life.

Julian was ready for that. Back in Miami, he had already searched for divorce lawyers in Chicago and narrowed it down to two. He called both. One of them struck the right chord, and they arranged a meeting. Julian went straight from the airport to the lawyer's office. The consultation was quick, almost effortless. His case was clear, straightforward. "Papers in two days," the lawyer said. "If both parties sign, you'll be free in thirty." Julian walked out, liking the man and liking the sound of the word free even more.

Julian quickly typed the message to Claire and hit send. Two minutes later, her reply flashed on the screen: *Sure. I wanted to meet too. We've got a ton to talk about. See you on Wednesday at the house.*

Julian smiled. She had no idea. No sense of the trap waiting for her. And this time, he promised himself, he would deliver the performance of his life.

Chapter 20

Claire pulled into the driveway, the same driveway she'd parked in for years, never once imagining she'd return as a guest. Yet here she was. Ironic, she thought. She had worked herself raw at the bank to build this life, only to snap one day, declare separation, and walk away.

Eight months ago. It felt like another lifetime.

At the front door, she froze. Wood and glass, an expensive door. But for her, it was the entrance into her old life, heavy with anger, frustration, and the ache of years lived wrong. Should she ring the bell like a stranger or break it the fuck down like it was still hers? Her mind said ring. Her heart said smash. She chose neither. She eased the door open and stepped inside. The first thing she saw was a bunch of cardboard boxes on the floor, which meant moving, leaving, ending. Some were full, some still empty.

"Julian?" she called.

"In the kitchen," his voice answered.

She followed it and found him at the counter, a book open in his hands. He looked up casually. "Hey, Claire."

"Hi, Julian. How have you been?" She slid onto the stool across from him, her eyes wandering. The house breathed ghosts at her with familiar walls, familiar smells. Memories came back, flooding like unwelcome guests.

"Are you moving or something?" Claire asked, motioning to the cardboard boxes.

"In fact, I am," Julian replied, voice flat, stripped of emotion. She didn't push further. After a pause, he asked, "What did you want to talk about?"

"Plenty. But since you called this meeting, let's start with you," she said evenly.

"You're not the boss here anymore, Claire," he shot back, looking straight at her.

"I never was," she replied.

"Really?" His tone carried the calculated bite of someone itching for a fight.

She shook her head, half in disbelief. "At least I wasn't the one who planted a passport in the car just to 'find' it and play the savior." She watched his face carefully, waiting for the flicker of guilt, the denial, the tell.

"What the hell are you talking about?" His voice rose, but she could see her torpedo had landed.

"You know exactly what I'm talking about. Same as the camera equipment your late uncle supposedly sold you when it was actually a gift."

"Oh…" he sneered. "So that's where you're going. You show up here with some fantasy about your passport that I helped you find, and gossip about my uncle, who changed his story daily. Gift, sale, gift again, he couldn't decide."

"Eventually, you never paid for it," she said coolly.

His hand slammed the counter, glass trembling. "No, I didn't!" His voice hit a shout, his jaw tightened. The warning signs of something brewing. "So what? What's the crime in that?"

"Nothing, Julian. Except the lies."

"My lies?" He laughed bitterly. "Give me a break, Claire. I did everything for you. I gave you freedom to chase your career while I took care of the house, of Chloe, of everything else. You came home to order, to dinner on the table, to your child smiling. I drove her to school, to practice, to friends. And you? You came home late, kissed her goodnight, and called that motherhood."

"I worked, Julian! Everything we have came from that work, from the bank. Someone had to shoulder the strain."

"Exactly!" His eyes flared. "When we met, you were already climbing the ladder. Would it have been smart to quit and ruin that? No. So I sacrificed. I killed myself day and night. I threw away my own career for you, for this family! And what did you do? You had the audacity to ask me that question. And then you left. Because what? I wasn't man enough? Come on, Claire! Someone had to raise our daughter. Someone had to run the house. And it sure as hell wasn't you!"

Claire stared at him, stunned. It was the first time she had seen Julian like this, furious, uncoiled, throwing his rage at her like a weapon. He drained a glass of water, steadied his voice, and said, "I've thought about all of this. I've made my decision."

He slid a stack of papers across the counter with a slow, theatrical push, like he was laying down the winning hand in a card game. "Here. Divorce. Uncontested. I waive every asset we own. I don't want a dime. Not from you. Not after what you did to me. You're a monster, Claire. Do you know that?"

Her throat tightened. She hadn't expected this. He wanted out, clean, final, without a fight.

"How are you going to live?" she managed to ask.

"That's not your fucking concern," he snapped. "You wrecked our marriage, wrecked me. I'm leaving, and I don't want to hear your name again."

Claire stood as if to leave but lingered a moment. "Julian, all those years, I felt it. The lies. The way you shaped everything for yourself, not for me, not for us. You can deny the passport trick all you want, you can deny the photography fantasy, while your mother slipped you two grand every month. But the truth is, you created guilt, day after day. You made me believe my career existed on your shoulders. That my success was borrowed."

He waved her off, bitter. "You don't even realize how true that is."

Her eyes narrowed. "What do you mean?"

"Nothing," he muttered. "I don't want to talk about it. I want the divorce. Plain and simple. Take the papers. Show them to your lawyer. Sign them."

She looked at him one last time, then picked up the papers. At the door, she turned back.

"Two months ago, you came to my house and told me you loved me. That was six months after I asked that fucking question, after we separated. You clearly wanted our life back, I know that. Now you hate the guts out of me and hand me the divorce papers with this theatrical performance of yours... Julian... why don't you just tell the truth? What's going on?"

She held her breath for a beat and then said quietly, "Maybe one day you will. But I don't think you're brave enough for that." Then she left, the door shutting behind her with a thud. Her hands shook on the wheel as she drove back. She picked up her phone at a red light, scrolling through recent calls: Olivia. Antonio. Chloe. Mom. Bank. Her thumb hovered, then she set it down. Breathe, Claire. Just breathe.

***

She didn't sleep that night. She sat by the wide window watching the lake outside. It was black and restless just like her thoughts.

Antonio called. She let it ring. She couldn't speak to him now. He followed with a text—*Are you all right?*—but she left that unanswered, too.

Julian's move had stunned her. Divorce? Uncontested? She wasn't ready for that. Whenever she had pictured their separation turning final, she always imagined negotiation, the inevitable 50/50 split of assets, fair, predictable. But this? He was waiving everything. Walking away with nothing. Claire couldn't explain it. It didn't make any sense. Another woman would, at the very least, require resources. A place to live, a safety net. But Julian had asked for none of it. So then what? The thought began to gnaw at her: maybe his mental health was cracking. Maybe she had pushed him there. What if their separation had unstrung him, left him suffering in silence, and now this "clean exit" was his way of erasing her, their life, even their daughter? Had she started all of this? It struck her how fragile a life together really was. Years of building, weaving, compromising, shaping, and then one sharp moment could kill it all. A single word, a single gesture, a single truth too naked to swallow could pull a thread loose, and once it started, the fabric would never lie smooth again. She thought about all the decisions that had brought her here. Not just the big ones like marriage, career, or motherhood, but the small ones too. The late nights at the office, the silences she let stretch too long, the times she didn't ask, or didn't answer. Each seemed insignificant at the time, yet together they had bent the arc of her life.

She had been the architect of the separation. She went to that dinner, saw something, felt something, and then snapped, tearing her life apart. His, too. But why? Was there ever a good reason? Not one she could hold, only one she could feel. And that was the cruelest part because her own feelings shifted like the weather. One day, conviction. The next day, doubt. She kept turning it over—was she right, or had she destroyed something that could have been saved?

She didn't know. She might never know. She had wanted her life to change. And so it had with one single question. And that question, oh, God... reckless, intimate, humiliating, might have been the spark that lit the fuse. Or maybe it was only the moment when everything already burning finally became visible. She didn't know. By morning, hollow from the long hours of circling thoughts, she typed an email to her secretary: *Cancel everything for today. I'm sick. I'll be better tomorrow.*

***

Julian slept well. He was pleased with himself, how smoothly he had shifted the blame onto her, how noble he must have looked, saying, I want nothing from you. He was proud of that line. It gave him a sense of closure: a man unappreciated for his years of service simply walking away. And calling her a monster, yes, he savored that most of all. For reasons he couldn't fully name, he wanted her to carry the sting of it. "I wasn't lying. She is one. She just doesn't realize I created her that way." This thought brought him comfort.

Only one minor irritation remained: he had failed to mold her into the fake dominant wife he'd always craved. The irony still amused him that she never realized she'd been the one controlled all along. Now his path seemed clear. He would wait for her to sign, wait for the papers to move through the court. Then he would walk free with two million in his pocket and a new life to claim. Angela had already scheduled their meeting with the lawyer to finalize the escrow account. The money was there. All that remained was the signature. He knew Angela saw through him. She understood that service wasn't a weakness at all. It was survival. Claire never did. On the phone, Angela had teased that she expected gratitude. Oh, he would show it. Licking her boots or whatever else she demanded for two million dollars? To Julian, that sounded like a real bargain.

Chapter 21

Claire walked toward her car. The air was heavy, rain threatening. She felt worn out. The fatigue of a day packed with high-profile meetings at the bank sat in her bones, heavy and immovable. And on top of it all, she had signed the papers that morning and sent them to Julian. She had wanted a separation. He wanted a divorce. Now their marriage was almost officially over.

Knowing that brought no clarity, no relief. Everything still stung, unfinished, half-decided, half-spoken. Yet somewhere inside, she was slowly learning to live with the incompleteness. To let go of things left unsolved, unanswered. She had just reached her car when a familiar voice cut through the damp air.

"Been actively avoiding me, haven't you?" She turned. Antonio stood there, smiling. Claire found herself smiling back. "No, not really. Just… busy. Overwhelmed."

"I thought so," he said. "Fancy dinner tonight?"

She hesitated. "I'm not sure. I'm kind of wrecked, to be honest. Just signed my divorce papers this morning."

His smile evaporated. "I'm sorry," he said gently. Then, after a beat: "Dinner's too heavy, then. What you need is a wine tasting."

Claire let out a small laugh. "A wine tasting, you say?"

"All the therapy you'll ever need," he teased. She shook her head, amused despite herself. "All right. Let's do it." Antonio took her hand, and together they walked to his car.

***

"Why the fuck am I so drunk?" she whispered as they stepped out of the wine-tasting boutique three hours later.

"Why exactly are you whispering?" Antonio laughed, holding her hand. "I don't know," she said. "I feel like everyone's listening. Judging."

"Oh, don't worry about that." Antonio's smile was easy, teasing. "No one cares if Claire Winters, the symbol of sobriety herself, had a few too many tasting pours. They'll forgive you."

She shook her head, half in disbelief, half in agreement. He guided her carefully into his car, making sure her seatbelt clicked. She gave him a sleepy smile. By the time he circled to the driver's side and got in, she was already gone, head tilted, breath even.

Antonio looked at her face. It was calm, happy, radiant. Why did this woman make him feel what he felt? He couldn't name it exactly, only that she pulled him in like a magnet, the only one who seemed able to stand toe-to-toe with him, to match his energy, to feel like a true partner. He glanced at her again, smiled, and started the engine.

***

Claire woke with a start. This wasn't her room. The walls were strange, painted in muted earth tones, and the sheets smelled faintly of cedar and something clean, something masculine. Her head throbbed. She sat up too quickly and realized she was wearing a T-shirt that didn't belong to her, soft cotton, too big, clearly a man's.

Her stomach lurched. What the hell? She flung the blanket back, searching for clues. Alone. She was alone in bed. No Antonio. Relief came, but it was tangled with panic. She rubbed her temples, trying to remember. Wine. Too much wine. His car. The steady hum of the engine. Then nothing.

"Good morning, Sleeping Beauty."

Her head snapped toward the doorway. Antonio stood there, grinning, a tray balanced in his hands: two coffees, two croissants dusted with icing sugar.

"Where am I?" she demanded, sharper than she meant.

"My place. Calm down," he said lightly, setting the tray on the nightstand. "No dungeons, no handcuffs. Just clean sheets and a T-shirt that looks better on you than on me."

Claire narrowed her eyes. "So you... undressed me?"

Antonio raised both hands in mock surrender. "Guilty. But only for humanitarian reasons. You fell asleep in your dress, shoes, and all. I wasn't about to let you spend the night like a collapsed mannequin."

Her face flushed. "And?"

"And nothing." His grin softened into something gentler. "I undressed you down to what a gentleman should. Then I gave you the shirt. And then, Claire Winters, you face-planted into the pillow and started snoring like a little bulldog."

Her mouth fell open. "I do not snore."

"Oh, you do. Adorably. I almost recorded it." He leaned against the wall, clearly enjoying himself. She laughed, shaking her head. "You're insufferable."

"And yet," he said, lifting her coffee toward her, "you'll drink this because you need it."

She took it, their fingers brushing briefly. He was right, and the first sip did feel like salvation.

"And just to be clear," Antonio added, serious now, "we didn't have sex. I wouldn't do that to you, drunk. When we do, I want you awake for every second of it."

Her cheeks burned, but she smiled into her cup. "Confident, aren't you?"

"Optimistic," he corrected, tearing a croissant in half and handing her a piece. "Don't confuse the two."

An hour later, he drove her home. The rain had passed, and the streets were glistening. She sat in the passenger seat, watching the city slide by, turning his words over in her head. For the first time, Claire let herself imagine it. A relationship. Dating Antonio. The thought both frightened and warmed her, and she didn't know which feeling was stronger.

***

The bravado dissolved, giving way to depression. Richard hadn't expected that. For all he knew about Angela, for all the warnings he'd ignored, his heart still ached. Life with her had been wild, full, intoxicating, even if the woman beside him was no moral compass. Far from it.

The drinking took over. He skipped days at the bank. The house, once charged with her presence, now felt cavernous, stripped. In his clearer moments, he reminded himself: she was a vulture, a woman who never loved him, only waited for the right moment to strike. But the memories betrayed him. Her body, her scent, the thrill of her games that made his skin crawl and his blood rush at the same time. He couldn't shake them. He didn't know what came next. He had imagined life would simply resume with Angela gone, everything else intact. Instead, it all felt broken.

Richard knew she was history. Angela had blackmailed him. Trust was gone, the case closed. Still, he craved her. A paradox of mind, heart, and body.

The doorbell rang. Richard jerked upright, shuffled off the sofa, and opened the door. "Hey there," Matthew said, stepping in, fresh and businesslike. Richard's oldest friend gave him a long look. "Hmm. Aren't you drowning your sorrows in whiskey, Rich?"

"I am, in fact." Richard's eyes were bloodshot, his hair unkempt. "Fuck it, Matthew, I'm trying to get her out of my system. But it takes time."

Matthew sat down, opened his briefcase, and pulled out a few documents. "Straight from the court. You're a free man now."

Richard smirked, but the relief was hollow. "Thanks," he muttered.

"So," Matthew asked, settling back. "What's the plan?"

"No plan. Honestly? I don't know what to do. And worse, work doesn't appeal to me right now. I've skipped days."

Matthew studied him for a moment. "I've been thinking about you, Richard. Not as your lawyer. As your friend. Want my two cents?"

Richard shrugged. "Always. When haven't I listened to you?"

"Right. So tell me, if you sold your stake in the bank today, what would you walk away with?"

Richard scratched his head. "Maybe forty."

"And everything else, stash, investments?"

"Another eight." He gave a bitter smile. "Used to be twenty, until a few weeks ago."

Matthew waved it off. "Don't brood over those twelve. Think of them as buying your freedom from the mess. And this house?"

"Five, maybe five and a half."

"Okay," Matthew said, quick with the math. "So you're sitting on roughly fifty million. Park forty million somewhere safe, you know how. That nets you two million a year, absolutely risk-free. Have you ever thought about it, Rich? Sun, beach, margaritas, beautiful women. Maybe you meet someone new, maybe you even find love again. But more than that, you will find calm. Stress-free life. Health. Peace. That's what makes you live longer, buddy. Calm."

Richard stared at him, incredulous. "What? Get rid of the bank? The job? My status? And what, become a beach bum?" But he didn't say it aloud. He only nodded, swallowing hard. They talked a little longer, then Matthew left. Richard poured himself another glass, stared at the liquid, and sipped slowly. Thoughts buzzed in his head like restless bees. Beach, huh?

Chapter 22

Julian walked into the office building, climbed to the third floor, and froze. The lawyer's office door was locked. The nameplate was gone. Angela was nowhere in sight. They had agreed to meet here. He dialed her number. A metallic operator's voice cut through: This number is no longer in service.

"What the fuck..." His pulse spiked, sweat breaking out across his forehead. Then his back went cold. He sprinted downstairs to reception. The clerk, indifferent, told him the office had been rented for a single month by someone from San Francisco. No, they didn't have details. And even if they did, they wouldn't share them. Policy.

Julian ran back upstairs, staring at the empty door, the blank wall where the nameplate had been. His throat tightened. The silence screamed what he couldn't yet accept. He had been played.

He pressed his palms flat against the wall, as if some hidden door might open if he begged hard enough. For weeks, he had built his fantasies around this moment—beaches, freedom, the smug smile he'd wear when Claire realized what he'd pulled off. Now it collapsed in front of him. The two million had never existed for him; it had been

Angela's mirage all along, a cruel little carrot dangled before a donkey too desperate to stop chasing.

The shame bit deeper than the loss. He had strutted in front of Claire with his "noble" sacrifice, convinced he'd fooled her, convinced he looked powerful, untouchable. But here he was, a man conned, discarded like trash, stripped even of the lies he once hid behind. He thought of all the times he'd knelt willingly, craving humiliation, but this was different. This wasn't chosen. This was real.

The two million dollars evaporated in an instant. The uncontested divorce, approved out of court just two days ago, now looked like the biggest blunder of his life. He had nothing. Nothing but a dingy motel room he could barely afford. Angela's twenty grand was nearly gone.

Julian slid to the floor and cried. Long, muffled sobs, the kind that sounded like a man attending his own funeral with tears spilling even though he was already dead. This was it. The end. Crushed, defeated, humiliated, he staggered to his feet and stumbled out of the building. He drifted aimlessly down the street, hollow, hating everyone—Angela, Claire, Richard, the whole damned world. His chest tightened; his blood ran hot. Desperation and fury tangled inside him until he grabbed his phone, scrolled through the numbers, and pressed one. When the line clicked open, he said the only word left to him. "Mom?"

***

The woman who had engineered Julian's spectacular downfall was, at that very moment, gliding across the Golden Gate Bridge. Angela was home again, San Francisco at her feet.

She drove a brand-new, flashy car, en route to a spa appointment. Rich now, yes, but hardly finished. Silicon Valley teemed with possibilities: ambitious men, dazzled men, men with appetites bigger than their caution. They were always the same. Hungry. Arrogant. Easy to bend if you stroked the right part of their ego. All she needed was to pick better this time. Another deal like Richard's, and she could retire to Mexico, Bali, or anywhere else that's cheap and beautiful. Not yet, though. Another five or six years of marriage seemed about right. Five years of fun. What she needed was someone with Richard's hunger for sex, for play, for excess. With that, her days would stay bright, colorful, and comfortable. She loved the thrill of a fresh adventure.

Her thoughts flicked to Julian, and she smirked. What an idiot. He'd really believed she'd hand him his money. Naïve didn't even begin to cover it. Still, she had to admit he'd been a useful idiot, a good servant. Perhaps, if she ever got bored, she'd summon him again. Dogs, after all, never forget who fed them. Traffic crawled. Angela checked the time. Eleven minutes left before the spa. She leaned back, adjusted the mirror, and let the city shimmer around her. God, she loved San Francisco.

***

Raindrops streaked down the window, leaving uneven signatures of a restless day. Claire sat across from Olivia, her chair angled toward the glass, watching the water trace its slow descent.

"So, how does it feel to be free of marriage?" Olivia asked. Claire smiled faintly. "Mixed, honestly. At first, I kept asking myself if what I did was right. If I really had enough to call it a dead end." She paused, weighing her words. "I mean, I acted mostly on a feeling. Not on hard evidence. It wasn't like Julian was caught with someone else, you know…"

Olivia's voice softened, but carried weight. "Let me tell you something. Yes, you acted on a feeling. But you were right to. Because if something in you insists it's wrong, it is. That's how growth happens. That's how you move toward a better life. A better you."

Claire lifted her cup. The coffee tasted good. Really good. The last few days had been calm, steady, almost in rhythm with her. She hadn't seen Antonio since that night in his T-shirt, drunk and asleep in his bed, but she planned to. She had a good feeling about him. She'd spoken to Chloe when the court papers arrived. Chloe seemed relieved, even happy for her. She said Julian claimed to be happy as well.

"So, what's next?" Olivia asked, leaning in. "You can start fresh now."

"Yes." Claire smiled. "But I don't feel rushed. I plan to take my time. I plan to live." Then she hesitated, shook her head as if she'd just made a decision. "Can I tell you a secret?"

Olivia tilted her hands open, offering space for whatever Claire needed to place there. "That's exactly why you're here." She smiled.

Claire drew in a long breath. "I shouldn't say this, but... I miss Amanda."

***

Later that night, Claire replayed what she'd told Olivia. She did miss Amanda. That much was true. But she also knew she'd never interfere with

Amanda's choices. Amanda had gone where she believed she belonged, living her life on her own terms. And that was fine. In a way, Amanda mirrored Claire herself: a woman who had chosen separation, who stepped into uncertainty because it felt necessary. Amanda claimed her own path. So had she.

Her thoughts drifted, slowly, inevitably, to Antonio. He was taking up more and more space in her mind, edging closer to her heart. There was something steady about him, a balance she craved. He could play, yes, but he was also stable, predictable, grounded. That mattered. She didn't want dull, like life with Julian had been, but she didn't want to be consumed by fire either. Balance. That was the word she kept circling back to.

Maybe she would enjoy power games one day and surrender the next. Maybe she wanted to try, to experiment, to live as fully as she could. And maybe Antonio was the one who could walk that line with her. At least Jamaica suggested so. Claire picked up her phone, typed a message, and pressed send: *Next Friday, my place. 8 p.m. I cook.* The reply came almost instantly: *Already thinking about the wine choice. That's on me. Need help in the kitchen?* Claire laughed, tapped out a laughing emoji, and added: *I'm not that bad.*

Chapter 23

Claire's week began with a jolt. An email from the Board pinged into her inbox Monday morning, stamped urgent. She was to attend a Board meeting on Friday at 10 a.m. No agenda, no explanation, just her presence required. Shit. The same Friday, she had promised Antonio she'd cook. That small, intimate promise had carried her through the last days, and now the Board was intruding. She considered asking Antonio if he knew anything. He was, after all, one of their most significant investors, but the thought made her stomach knot. It would look weak, unprofessional. No, she would walk in blind if she had to.

To make matters worse, Richard called that morning. His voice was smooth, careful, almost too polite. "Can you meet me today? Early evening, say five-thirty? A business dinner. Best if we meet in a more... relaxed atmosphere. Not office." She agreed automatically, though her gut tightened. Something was brewing, and she didn't like the smell of it.

By late afternoon, Antonio still hadn't called. Unusual for him. Claire felt the edges of unease sharpening. Maybe she was paranoid, maybe she wasn't. She buried herself in work, meetings stacked, her calendar jammed with numbers, reports, and signatures. Keep moving, she told herself. Don't spiral. Don't panic.

She arrived at the restaurant five minutes early, determined to look composed. But Richard was already there, seated by the window, a glass of wine in front of him.

She paused, studying him before he noticed her. Something about him was off. For anyone watching, he seemed calm, even relaxed, but Claire knew better. She noticed that his body carried a strange tension like a man waiting for a jury to file back into the courtroom and announce whether he would walk free or spend the rest of his life in chains.

"Claire," he greeted warmly as she sat.

"Richard."

He offered her a glass of red. She accepted. They ordered starters and spoke of nothing of consequence until the waiter disappeared. Then Richard reached for his briefcase. He withdrew a single sheet of paper, slid it across the table, and placed his hand lightly on top of it for a moment before letting go.

"Claire," he said evenly, "this is a photocopy of the Board's minutes regarding your appointment as VP of Operations. It's dated. Logged properly in the documents." She looked down. The seal, the signatures, the structure of the minutes, it all looked correct. She had seen it before, months ago, when the appointment was confirmed. Nothing unusual at first glance. Lifting her eyes to his, she waited.

"I want you," he said, his tone lower now, "to remember the date of that appointment. It's important for the rest of our conversation."

Claire nodded slowly, though she didn't know why. A strange chill passed through her. Richard was acting unlike himself: composed but taut, rehearsed but unsettled, as though bracing for impact. He looked at her for a second too long, as if steadying himself on her gaze, then spoke.

"I've submitted my resignation to the Board. Late last week. Along with it, I negotiated the sale of my shares."

Claire's breath caught. Words rushed to her lips, but tangled, never forming. Her mouth opened, then closed, useless. Her eyes, though, widened. Richard didn't pause. His voice was measured, careful. "I also advised the Board to appoint you as the next President of the Bank. That's why you're being called in on Friday."

The air between them went thin. Claire finally found a fragment of speech. "Oh my God! What's going on, Richard?"

The impact of his words shattered her balance. It was the last thing she ever expected to hear from him. "Well…" He shifted slightly in his chair, his shoulders rising then falling like a man who'd played this moment in his head a hundred times and still found himself unprepared. "It's quite a story. And yes, it involves you. Bear with me, Claire. I'll tell you all of it. Piece by piece."

She nodded, shocked and silent. Something about him was different, stripped, raw. Richard picked up his napkin, wiped at his mouth, though he hadn't eaten a bite. He lowered it again, then began.

"About five, maybe six weeks ago, I divorced Angela."

The words dropped like a bomb between them. Claire's chest clenched. Again, she almost blurted out a reaction, but she forced herself to swallow it back. She only stared. He gave her a crooked, bitter smile. "Yes. A surprise for me too. I thought I loved her. Maybe I did. Maybe I still do. She... well... not so much, as it turned out."

His voice lowered. His eyes, unblinking, locked on hers. "Claire, I've lived as a corrupt man. Flawed. Arrogant. Cunning. Sometimes monstrous. And Angela... she knew all of that. She played it like a conductor with her orchestra. She fed it. We did terrible things together. We treated people like toys, trash. Took advantage. Broke rules. Broke people. And it felt like fun. Angela made it fun."

He paused, his throat tightening.

"She was... a goddess, really. A goddess of sex, of power, of humiliation, and control. She knew which buttons to press. God help me, she always knew." His voice cracked on the last word. "And she kept pressing them."

Silence fell. The restaurant's soft hum, the faint clink of cutlery, the low murmur of other conversations, suddenly sounded distant, unreal.

Then Richard's voice came again, quieter this time. "One of those buttons touched you. Touched your family. And, Claire—" He leaned forward now, his hand flat on the table as if anchoring himself. "I am... very, very sorry for what I've done. I truly am. That's why I want to come clean. I want out of this mess. I want to carry on with my life without the burdens of the past."

Claire felt the blood drain from her face. Her pulse hammered in her throat. She couldn't hold back any longer. "What exactly do you mean, Richard?" she demanded, her voice sharper than she intended. "How is my family involved?"

And then he told her.

Piece by piece, like a man unspooling a noose around his own neck. The studio. The champagne flowing since morning, glasses refilled as though they were part of the air. The three of them, Richard, Angela, and Julian, buzzing, loose, blurred at the edges. He described the way Julian's eyes kept drifting, hungry, to Angela's body as she shifted poses for the camera. How Angela fueled it deliberately, tossing out filthy comments, every line sharper than the last, her voice laced with seduction and cruelty.

Julian had giggled at her jokes, nervous, boyish, like a man already surrendering without knowing it. And then came the whisper. Angela, leaning close, her breath warm against Richard's ear, sliding the words into him like poison wrapped in silk.

He admitted it. He'd followed her instructions. A fool, he called himself, and worse. He'd lied to Julian. Lied because he could. Lied because Angela told him to. Lied even though he knew the truth that the Board had already made its decision, that Claire's appointment was signed, sealed, and logged. None of it had ever depended on Julian. But he lied anyway. Lied, then leveraged it, and blackmailed Julian into submission. Pressed him into Angela's hands. Well, thighs, to be exact.

"Yes, we were all drunk," Richard said, his face drawn tight, eyes shadowed. "All three of us. But that's no excuse. Not for what I did." Claire's body went rigid. When he said the words aloud—Julian kneeled in front of Angela—something snapped.

"Fuck you, Richard!" Claire spat, her voice cutting across the restaurant like a whip. The restaurant stilled for a second. A fork clattered somewhere, and the waiter froze mid-step, caught in the shockwave of her words. Claire didn't care. Let them all hear. Let them all watch. Richard didn't flinch. He only lowered his gaze, shook his head once, slowly. Then he lifted it again, his eyes bleak but steady. "You have every right to say that. I expected it. But I must finish."

He leaned closer across the table, his voice confessional. "Claire... that's not the end of the story. Before you start feeling sorry for your ex, before you waste your pity, you need to hear all of it."

Claire's heart jumped. Her voice rose, sharp with disbelief. "What do you mean? What end? What else is there?"

"As I said, two months ago, Angela asked me for a divorce." Richard's eyes narrowed as if reliving it. "But not just asked, Claire. She put it bluntly: Pay up, or the studio scene goes to Claire, and your reputation is ruined." Claire felt her stomach drop.

"And do you know when she chose to drop that little bomb?" Richard continued. "Right after she realized you and Antonio had a past. Or a present. Or maybe a future. I don't know which, but she used it. She calculated that with Antonio behind you, you could ruin me. And she was right about that."

He let the words hang before leaning in closer. "But here's the trick. She told me she had enlisted Julian in her project. Said she controlled everything now. Those were her exact words: I control him. And then she asked for twelve million dollars as her divorce settlement." Claire's eyes widened, her heart kicking against her ribs. Then it struck her, sharp, undeniable, like a slap. Holy shit.

That was why Julian had been so bold. So smug. So arrogant with his clean little waiver of assets, with his theatrics of nobility. He wasn't walking away empty-handed at all. He knew he was in on Angela's scheme. He knew he'd get his slice. Her voice cracked. "And?"

Richard exhaled, long and weary. "And I paid, Claire. Twelve million. She signed the papers, and I got the divorce." Claire blinked rapidly, trying to keep up. She signed the papers, too. Richard went on.

"Then I sat with it. For weeks. At first, I told myself I was free. But slowly, something shifted. I decided to change my life. I quit the bank. I'm heading south. Sun, sea, no boardrooms. Maybe I'll drown in tequila instead of quarterly reports. That's going to be my life now. Escape, not empire." He gave a humorless laugh, then lifted one finger, as if asking her not to interrupt.

"But before I let go completely, I hired a private investigator to follow both of them." He reached for his briefcase. "Here's what I know."

He slid a small envelope across the table.

"They met twice at a so-called lawyer's office. Except the man wasn't a lawyer. No license, no record, no bar admission under that name. Just smoke and mirrors. Julian stayed at a run-down motel outside the city. And one day, the PI followed him back to that office only to find the door locked, the nameplate gone, and the lawyer vanished. The setup dismantled overnight."

Claire's hands trembled as she opened the envelope. Photographs spilled out with grainy shots of Julian slumped on a hallway floor, his face buried in his hands, his body wracked in visible despair. In one, his phone lay just out of reach on the carpet, as if he'd dropped it mid-collapse. In another, his knees buckled inward, not like a man sitting but like someone too defeated to stand. Claire's stomach twisted. Richard's voice cut through her disbelief. "It broke him, Claire. Crashed him completely. She played him. Just like she played me. Must have promised him cash—how much, I don't know—but gave him nothing." He leaned back, studying her reaction. "You probably know he's moved back to his mother's house."

Claire's throat closed. A whisper escaped before she could stop it. "No. I didn't know that."

The words barely left her lips. She couldn't believe what she was hearing. Her mind flashed back to the snapshots from that fateful dinner. And now it all made sense. Every piece fell into place. They had known the secret. All three of them. Richard, Angela, Julian. She had been the odd one out. But she had felt it. God, she had felt it. The sickness of it, the wrongness humming beneath every touch, every silence. She let the photographs slip from her fingers and rest on the table between them. For a long moment, neither of them spoke. Then, Claire straightened in her chair, her eyes locking on Richard's.

"You all thought you were playing games," she said, her voice almost calm. "But the truth is, the game was always playing you. Angela. Julian. You. None of you ever saw the cost until it came due. And now it's too late. You wanted to come clean? Fine. You did. But don't mistake that for redemption. You're not walking away clean, Richard. You're just walking away."

She pushed the envelope back toward him, rose from her seat, and lifted her bag. Her heart was pounding, but her steps were sure. Richard stayed still, the pictures lying like evidence of his own undoing. Claire walked out of the restaurant without looking back.

Chapter 24

The apartment was silent. Just the hum of the refrigerator and the muted rhythm of the rain against the glass. Claire sat curled on the sofa, whiskey glass in hand, shoes still on, her jacket draped loosely over her shoulders like a shield she had forgotten to take off. Richard's words replayed in her head, not as sentences anymore, but as fragments, jagged pieces she was now fitting into a complete picture: Angela's whisper. Julian kneeling. Twelve million. Lies. Games. She let her head fall back and closed her eyes.

Julian. God, Julian. For years, she had let his softness fill the gaps, telling herself his devotion was love, even when a part of her felt it was simply another form of control. He hadn't struck her, hadn't cheated, hadn't screamed. Instead, he had built a quiet system around her, one made of sighs, omissions, and guilt. He hadn't chosen her career for her. No, she had clawed her way up the bank herself. But he had found a way to script it as his sacrifice, his gift, his burden. He made her success feel borrowed, like something she owed. Drop by drop, he had shaped the air until guilt became her native language. And she'd called it marriage.

Now she saw it clearly, painfully. The lies were never just about passports or equipment, or money hidden and stories invented. The greater lie was the one they both inhabited: the illusion that she was free, when in truth she had been managed, molded, handled, and taught to believe she wanted the very life that had been chosen for her, even though it had been hers all along.

And then came the studio. She hadn't been there, but Richard's confession painted it in unbearable clarity: the grotesque theatre dressed up as loyalty. Julian's words came back to her, sharp as glass: "You don't even realize how true that is." That was what he'd thrown at her when she said her success had always felt handed down. Now she understood. He had twisted his own private humiliation into her debt, weaving a story where her achievements existed on his shoulders. Knees, actually. He had made her believe she owed him for the very life she had built herself. That was his trick. The quiet theft of her pride.

Claire took a sip, and it burned like fire, sharp, searing, bitter, like the taste of her old life. The picture Richard had painted made her nauseous. She could see it too clearly—Julian in front of Angela ... servicing her.

Angela. She was a hunter, yes, but at least she was half-honest about it. She played with knives in the open. Richard? Broken, but trying to be transparent now in a way Julian had never been. And Julian... he was the cruelest paradox of all. A man who called himself a servant, but who mastered the art of quiet domination.

Claire stood and paced the room, her glass of whiskey trembling slightly in her hand. For the first time since that infamous dinner, she didn't feel lost in questions. She didn't feel guilty for asking, for snapping, for breaking the life they had built. She felt strangely clean. The separation had not been madness. It had been survival. It had been the one honest act in a marriage built on fictions. She hadn't ruined her life. She had saved it. And the irony, sharp and bitter as the single malt, was that it took Richard, the last man she would have ever trusted, to confirm what her instincts had whispered all along.

Claire stopped at the window, gazing at the slick streetlights shimmering on wet pavement. Somewhere out there, Julian was back at his mother's house, stripped of illusions, of money, of dignity. She should have felt pity. She tried to summon it. But none came. Not anymore. Tomorrow, she thought, she would test that resolve. Tomorrow, she would face him, not as his wife, not as his victim, but as herself.

***

It had been a couple of weeks at his mother's house. Humiliation came first, sharp and hot. Then depression. Then the long, suffocating stretch of reflection. His whole life now seemed absurd, unreal. A failure.

But it hadn't begun that way. No, once upon a time, it had worked. The years with Claire had been steady, comfortable. He lived a quiet life and performed his part. Yes, he serviced, deferred, let her shine, and he framed it all as devotion. But he liked it. He liked the predictability, the safety. Long, silent days while Claire killed herself at the bank and Chloe busied herself at school, Julian relished the quiet. He read. He cooked. He perfected recipes. He never wasted money. Even Claire's money. Not because he respected her work, but because he was fine with little. He didn't want more. Travel unsettled him, even frightened him. Social events exhausted him. Going out with Claire was avoided whenever possible, endured only when her complaints about boredom grew too loud. Home was his fortress. The outside world was chaos, and he fought hard to keep the walls intact.

And he lied for it. Manipulated for it. Kept Claire's guilt alive because guilt was his ally, the glue that held his small kingdom together. But now it was all gone. Memories. Ashes. He had been outplayed, humiliated, stripped bare by a professional of far higher caliber. He had deceived Claire. But Angela... Angela danced with men like Richard: powerful, dangerous, vulnerable. She'd consumed Julian like an appetizer.

His mother didn't ask questions. She simply offered him his old room and the use of her car. She asked if he needed money. He said no. He didn't know what he needed. Maybe all he craved for was this room and the quiet. His father had been dead for years, and now it was just the two of them, mother and son under the same roof. The thought tasted of regression, of retreat.

The photography business? Who knew. The studio was gone, the equipment stacked in boxes in the garage like relics of a dream. Maybe he could advertise online and do on-location shoots. Scrape something together.

The room hadn't changed. His childhood walls, the old desk, the narrow bed, it was as if no time had passed at all. And in a way, it hadn't. After a week, he slipped back into the pattern too easily: sleeping late, staring at screens, barely stepping outside. His mother worried aloud and told him to at least walk in the park. He promised he would. He never did. He hated that park.

That morning, he woke past ten. The house was empty. His mother had gone to visit her sister and would not be back until late afternoon. He opened his laptop and began fumbling through the setup of a Google Ads account, thinking maybe five hundred dollars could bring in a booking or two, maybe one decent photo shoot. Something. Anything.

Then the doorbell rang. He froze. Glanced through the window. Claire's car sat in the driveway. And Julian's heart sank.

He opened the door and met her eyes. In an instant, he knew that she knew. Everything. How she'd found out, he couldn't imagine, but the certainty struck like a hammer. His mind raced, flipping through his usual tricks, the little manipulations and rehearsed defenses. None of them would work here. Not this time. This time, he would have to improvise. He stepped back, gesturing her inside with the most depressed face he could master. "Hi."

"Hi," she echoed, her tone flat.

He spread his hands, palms open, a half-shrug that was equal parts surrender and performance as if telling her – that's it. I am back to square one. Then he gave her one of his tired little smiles, the kind that had always bought him sympathy before. One of his many in the arsenal of tricks.

"Is your mom home?" she asked.

"No. She won't be back for a few hours."

Claire walked into the living room and lowered herself onto the sofa. He followed, sitting across from her, his body too restless for stillness. "Tea?" he offered, desperate to fill the air.

"No, thank you." She cut through the courtesy. Her eyes locked on his. "How much did she promise you?"

His gaze dropped instantly. To the floor. Then back up. Then down again. Trapped. Finally, he let the truth slip out like a stone falling from his mouth. "Two million."

The silence between them sharpened. He swallowed hard. "Before you say anything, Claire... let me tell you the truth. All of it."

She studied him, her face steady, but inside she was gauging. Was this a confession, or another play? His slumped shoulders, his defeated eyes, they might have been masks too. She couldn't tell. She only nodded once. Continue.

Julian shifted in his seat, hands clasping and unclasping, and began. His voice was thin at first, but it gathered momentum as he went on.

"I know who I am, Claire. Who I've always been. Who I've spent my life hiding. I never told anyone this; you're the first because I've been afraid. Afraid every second of my life. Afraid of the world out there, that ugly world just waiting to punish me. I've always believed people would take advantage of me, humiliate me, abuse me if I let them too close." His breath hitched. His hands trembled as he pressed them flat against his knees. He drew in a deep breath, as though bracing himself for the blow of saying it out loud.

"It all started in school... When I was thirteen, maybe fourteen," Julian began, his voice low, "our school was divided. Two gangs. Two rival camps. And if you weren't in one of them, you were prey. I wasn't in either. So I was bullied. A lot. They'd wait for me in the park after school, shove me around, kick me, scatter my things across the ground like it was a game." He gave a hollow laugh. "For them, it was fun. For me, it was survival."

He leaned back, his eyes not quite meeting hers. "One day, I realized I couldn't keep living like that. I had to do something. So I came up with a plan. A daring one, at least for me. There was this guy — Jackson, a leader of the gang. Always carried a fancy leather wallet stuffed in his back pocket. I was quick with my hands, Claire. So I waited for the right moment. In the cafeteria, where the crowd pressed in close, I slipped it out. Stole it. Hid it away. Then I waited a couple of periods, letting him panic. Later, I walked up to him with the wallet in hand, told him I'd found it behind a trash can by the staircase."

Julian's mouth twisted at the memory. "He checked. Everything was there. And he actually thanked me. Then he looked me in the eye and asked if I wanted to be his runner. His personal dog, he called it. Smiling, like it was a joke. I agreed. The bullying stopped. I could breathe again. I could walk home without looking over my shoulder."

Claire's eyes narrowed. Her words were sharp. "So you did exactly the same thing with my passport, Julian."

He hesitated, then nodded. "Yes. I admit that. And I'm sorry for that, Claire. Sometimes... sometimes I wanted to be of service to you so badly that I created situations to be... of service."

She thought about it. No, that was a lie he told her. Or maybe it was a lie he told himself, too. What he really created were situations to gain leverage, to control by appearing indispensable. But she didn't say it aloud.

Julian went on, his voice dropping lower. "But it didn't stay that simple. Jackson wanted more. His throat went dry. "One day, after gym, when everyone else had gone, he lingered. I was picking up the balls, and he told me to—"

"Stop right there, Julian!" Claire's voice cracked, rising sharp enough to cut the air. "Stop! It hurts me just to hear it."

He closed his mouth, nodded quickly, almost like a scolded child.

"I get it," she said firmly. Then, after a beat, softer: "And I want to help you." Her hand went into her purse. For a fleeting, promising second, Julian's heart jumped, and he imagined her fetching a checkbook. But instead, she pulled out a small white card and slid it across the table.

"This is Olivia Dayton. Therapist. Call her. You need help, Julian." She stood. "That was actually the purpose of my visit."

Claire walked toward the door, then stopped, walked back. She pulled a folded paper from her purse and set it on the table in front of him.

"Richard told me everything," she said. "He resigned from the bank. And he also gave me this." Her hand lingered for a second on the paper before she let go. Julian's eyes followed, but he didn't reach for it.

"That," she continued, her voice precise, resolute, "is the Board's decision to appoint me VP of Operations. And look at the date, Julian. It's three days before your little escapade in the studio with Angela." Her words cut like ice.

"Richard played you. Just like Angela did. Your so-called 'service' to her had nothing to do with my career." She let that hang in the silence, her eyes steady on his. "So now you know. And if my word means anything to you, please, get help. I'll pay for your sessions with Olivia. That's all I can do for you, Julian." Then she turned, opened the door, and left without another word.

***

Claire drove to work with Julian's story looping in her mind like a film reel she never wanted to see. Was he truly that damaged? Had he really endured that kind of humiliation at school, the kind of trauma that brands itself into the skin and never fully fades? Maybe. Maybe not. With Julian, truth had always been slippery, a shifting surface where you never quite knew what was solid and what was illusion.

And in the end, she realized, she didn't need to know. The marriage was behind her. She was free. What mattered now was not excavating the ruins of his past but making sure she didn't stumble back into them. Still, a trace of pity lingered. She had offered him something real this time. A lifeline, fragile but genuine. Whether he would take it or not was his choice, not hers. But she would not gamble on that.

***

A couple of days passed. Julian savored the memory of Claire's visit. He loved how he had slipped a seed of doubt into her mind. Maybe it was not enough for her to bite down fully, but very close to leaving her doubtful. That was good. Ambiguity was fertile ground, the beginning of a new game. He'd let it sit, germinate, and he would, maybe, harvest it later.

The sessions she mentioned? He planned to take them. Therapy could serve its purpose, but not in the way Claire imagined. He didn't want healing; he wanted refinement. Every conman studied his craft, and if a therapist could help him polish his performance, hone his control, then why not? He would emerge sharper, stronger. More dangerous. And Claire was paying for it.

He almost admired himself for how quickly he had spun the story. So pitiful, so bulletproof. A performance stitched together from fragments of truth, just enough to be undeniable if she bothered to fact-check. Yes, there had been a Jackson at school. Yes, there had been gangs, two rival camps that made life hell for the stragglers. Yes, he had been bullied, often, mercilessly. But the wallet trick? The gym? Lies, every word of it. In reality, he had done nothing to fight back, nothing but wait out the years in silence, surviving through invisibility. Still, the story worked. It made him sound wounded, damaged, layered, and tragic. Exactly what he needed her to believe.

But Julian's little performance for Claire unraveled almost instantly, along with the promise of therapy sessions that would never be kept because someone else was already writing the rules of his life. As he filled the kettle and fiddled with the chipped mug in the kitchen, his phone buzzed on the counter. He glanced at the screen: unknown number. Curiosity prickled. He swiped it open.

Still want your money? You will have to beg me. Real hard.

Julian's lips curled into a slow, crooked smile. Angela. Relief rushed through him like a drug. She was still out there. Still watching. Still dangling the line. He hadn't been discarded altogether. He'd been summoned now. Tested. And begging... Oh, God... Begging was what he did best. If she wanted him on his knees, so be it. He'd crawl if that's what it took. Somewhere in that humiliation, there was hope. Hope for the money. Hope for a way back into her orbit. He tapped out one word with shaky fingers: *Anything.*

The message hung on the screen a second before sending, then it was gone, flying toward her like bait on a hook. He imagined her reading it, imagined her triumphant smile. Whether he was her pawn or she was his unsuspecting queen remained to be seen. What mattered was that the board was reset.

By the end of the week, following Angela's precise instructions, Julian rented a U-Haul, packed his equipment, and set off on a long drive to San Francisco. A new studio was waiting, one built for their games. Another house had already been chosen, destined to showcase a massive portrait of Angela, the masterpiece Julian would create with obsessive devotion.

***

Richard woke late, the tequila and the night's beach dancing still echoing through his head. He blinked to clear the fog and turned to the pillow beside him: a gorgeous tumble of blonde hair, his Swedish beauty, curled in sleep. Last night had been good, her body eager, the sex more than satisfying. But still… she was no Angela.

He reached for his phone, thumbed through messages and emails, and froze on the one he'd been waiting for. The private investigator's report from San Francisco laid out Angela's movements in careful, clinical detail, and it contained the crucial line: Julian had shown up on the scene, setting up a studio and moving in his equipment. The report made one thing clear: Angela had helped him. Together, they were definitely up to something.

Richard smiled, slow and cold. They'd settled into a new enterprise, and he would watch it closely before he struck. No one blackmailed Richard Pollak without consequence. He had no intention of letting this go. When Angela left, he set a budget, mapped every step, hired a private investigator firm, and waited. Let her build the stage, he thought, let her make the first mistakes. Now that she'd teamed with Julian, he'd watch them closely, play the comfortable beach bum, and stay hidden until they tangled themselves in a new web of deceit. Then he would move. And his revenge would be very sweet.

Chapter 25

Friday wrapped everything up. The Boardroom had been hushed, reverent almost, when the vote was cast. It passed unanimously. Claire Winters was appointed President of the Bank, effective immediately. One by one, the members rose, shaking her hand, offering smiles, congratulations, applause. Claire returned them all with measured poise, but inside she felt something shift — an arrival, a coronation of sorts. She had climbed. She had endured. And now she had reached the summit. For years, she had worked like a force of nature, proving herself, balancing tenacity with elegance, control with vision. Now the recognition came stamped with power, the power she knew she could wield, and wield well.

When she stepped into what was now her office, Antonio was waiting. He didn't rise at first. He stayed in her chair — her new chair — legs stretched out, arms resting on the leather as if testing the throne before she claimed it. When he finally stood, there was no smile, only an appraising look.

"President Winters," he said, his voice edged with irony.

Claire, sensing play, arched a brow theatrically, walked past him, and lowered herself into the chair he had warmed. She leaned back, folding her hands in her lap. He wanted to play, so let's play, she thought.

"That's Madam President to you," she smiled, mocking his tone. His lips twitched, but he didn't laugh. "Congratulations. Though I can't decide if you've won, or if Richard simply handed you this crown for a reason."

"Reason?" she asked lightly, though the word stung. Antonio leaned closer, palms flat on her desk, his eyes locked on hers. "I am no fool, Claire. Richard Pollak doesn't resign. Not unless he's forced. Not unless there's something... a scandal of sorts. And you... You were always very close to him. So tell me, Claire, did Richard hand you this crown, or did you take it off his corpse?"

She narrowed her eyes. "Jealousy doesn't really suit you, Antonio."

"Oh, I'm jealous," he admitted, his voice dropping lower. "Jealous of Richard, jealous of anyone who's had you before me. But don't confuse that with weakness. I know power when I see it. And I know you're hiding something about Richard, about all this setup."

"Richard... He's never had me, Antonio. Remember that." Her voice held just a sliver of steel. She paused and then added, "If you want me, you can have me, but only on my terms. Not yours."

The air thickened. For a long beat, they simply stared at each other, both unflinching, both daring the other to look away first. Finally, Antonio straightened, slow, steady. His smile returned, charming again, but his eyes stayed sharp.

"Tonight," he said, "you will cook for me. I'll bring the wine. And maybe... you'll tell me the truth. Or maybe you'll keep me guessing."

She tilted her head. "Maybe..."

"That's what I love about you," he said. Then he leaned down, close enough for her to feel the heat of his breath, and whispered, "But don't mistake me for one of your board members. I don't follow orders, Madam President, unless I want to." He took her hand and kissed it with a flourish, mocking and sincere at the same time, then walked out without looking back.

When the door closed, Claire sat still. The chair was still warm from him. That, she realized, was the point. He hadn't tested the leather. He'd tested her.

Sitting in her throne, letting her watch him do it. A question disguised as ease: Do you want a man who yields?

His jealousy had been a confession, yes, but also a tactic. Most men hid it. Antonio displayed it like a weapon laid on a table—visible and not to be mistaken for weakness. And that last line, 'I don't follow orders,' didn't land like defiance so much as a gauntlet. Not Julian's pliancy. Not Richard's coercion. Something riskier: a man who could pull against her without trying to pull her back down.

She felt the flicker of thrill and a prickle of caution in the same breath. If he was testing sovereignty, so was she. Would he crowd her crown or steady it? Would he demand intimacy as tribute, or earn it? She wouldn't explain Richard. Not tonight. Explanation was a tax the powerful paid to keep the peace. She had no interest in paying it.

She glanced at the nameplate on the desk. It said President Claire Winters, then to the door he'd just walked through. Tonight's dinner would be a diagnostic. She'd set the tempo, the spacing, the rules, softly, invisibly, and see whether Antonio sensed the wire. If he pushed, she'd push back harder. If he held the line without flinching, maybe he was worth the truth, piece by piece. If not, she would enjoy the wine and send him home with a smile. The question wasn't whether Antonio followed orders; it was whether he could meet them without being told. That, she decided, was the difference between a partner and a project.

She thought of the months behind her. The lies. The betrayals. The end of her marriage. The rediscovery of herself. Brutal, yes, but also a crucible. Each cut had left scars, but also steel. Each storm had stripped her, carved her, and left her sharper. This was her life now. Her rules. Her throne.

She picked up her bag, ready to shop, to cook, to prepare for Antonio. To test him. To see if he could handle the woman she had become.

Her phone buzzed. A new message lit the screen: *I am now free for real and yours if you take me back. Amanda.*

Claire froze. Her heart skipped a beat. Then a slow, dangerous smile curved her lips. Perfect, just perfect. Antonio was waiting at her table. Amanda was walking back into her life just as Claire had predicted. Her name now gleamed on the President's door. Julian was crawling in his ruins. It was more than a victory for her. It was power with its raw, intoxicating edges. Her own power.

Sliding into her car, she stared at the message again for a few long seconds. Thoughts jumped. Antonio needed to be tested. Amanda was the perfect litmus. Claire smiled and typed: *Can you make it for dinner tonight? 8 pm. My place.* As the engine purred to life, she whispered to her own reflection in the glass: Time to write my own rules. A screen blinked back: *On my way.*

***

Printed in Dunstable, United Kingdom